USBORNE

TRUE STORIES OF
SURVIVAL

PAUL DOWSWELL

CONTENTS

RENFREWSHIRE COUNCIL	
196099821	
Bertrams	26/08/2015
904	£5.99
GLE	

Dive to disaster

Just off the coast of New Hampshire, USA, the submarine *Squalus* (pronounced Skway-lus) sailed briskly along the surface of the Atlantic Ocean. It was 8:40am, on May 23, 1939. Brand new, *Squalus* was undergoing sea-trials before she was delivered to the US Navy.

As she cut through the choppy sea, her captain, 35-year-old Lieutenant Oliver Naquin, stood face to the wind and spray on the conning tower. The previous 19 test dives he had carried out with his ship had all gone to plan, but the next procedure would test both the 56 men in his crew, and their vessel, to the limit. *Squalus* was about to carry out a practice crash-dive, an emergency procedure where a submarine under attack on the surface submerges as quickly as possible.

Naquin called down to his radio operator, ordering him to report their position to the submarine's home port of Portsmouth, New Hampshire. When he was satisfied all was well, he took one final breath of salty sea air then hit a button on the bridge which sounded the crash dive alarm.

As a klaxon reverberated around the narrow ship, he hurried below to the control room, closing the upper and lower tower hatches as he climbed down into the depths of the submarine.

Inside the control room, men stood alert by dials and instruments, immersed in the intricate sequence of events that would take his submarine smoothly under the water.

Naquin called out a series of well-rehearsed commands:
"Secure all vents."
"Rig sub for diving."
"Flood main ballast tanks one and two."
"Open valves – bow buoyancy tanks."
"Main tanks three to seven – stand by."

Everything was going like clockwork. Standing next to Naquin was his chief officer Lieutenant Walter Doyle. His eyes were glued to an instrument panel known as the "Christmas tree". As all outside vents and hatches were closed, a set of indicator lights changed from red to green to show that the ship was sealed against the sea.

Naquin caught Doyle's eye and smiled briskly. The ship's ballast tanks rapidly filled with water, and *Squalus* swiftly sank to 15m (50ft). On the surface, less than a minute after Naquin had sounded the alarm, all was calm. It was as if the submarine had never been there.

❖

Squalus settled underwater and Naquin and Doyle congratulated themselves on a successful operation. But then a strange fluttering in Naquin's ears made him startle, and he realized immediately that something terrible was happening to his ship.

An instant later, a terrified sailor looked up from an intercom and shouted, "The engine room is flooding!" Naquin gave the order to surface immediately. Compressed air hissed into the flooded ballast tanks and the stricken submarine began to rise. Her bow broke the surface, but tons of water were now cascading into the rear of the ship. The weight in her stern dragged her sharply down, and *Squalus* was swallowed by the sea.

Inside was mayhem. In flickering light, tools, fittings, even torpedoes, unhinged by the steep angle of the dive, rained down on hapless sailors. Those who had not anchored themselves in a secure perch, tumbled along the ship and into bulkheads that separated each compartment. In the flooding rear section of the submarine, soaking men struggled to escape before heavy, steel, watertight doors were slammed shut to block off the rising torrent.

Sea water now rushed into the network of interconnecting pipes that ran throughout the submarine, and jets of water spurted over men and equipment from bow to stern. Along the length of the ship, the crew struggled desperately to seal air and communication pipes.

❖

As *Squalus* sank, another catastrophe threatened to destroy the ship before it even hit the bottom. In the forward battery room, ranks of batteries, which powered the vessel when she was underwater, were threatening to explode and blow the submarine to fragments.

Acrid blue sheets of flame flashed across the room, and spitting white arcs of electricity crackled from terminal to terminal. With extraordinary courage, chief electrician Lawrence Gainor thrust his arm into the guts of the submarine's electrical machinery and shut off the power supply. One disaster at least had been averted, but now *Squalus* had been plunged into complete darkness.

With the lights off and the contents of the submarine beginning to settle, *Squalus* continued to drift to the sea bottom in eerie silence. Inside, each man, alone in his black topsy-turvy world, waited dumbfounded for the impact to come. Every one of the crew, from Naquin downward, could only pray that when their ship hit the ocean floor it would not split open like a bursting balloon.

Squalus sinking toward the ocean floor

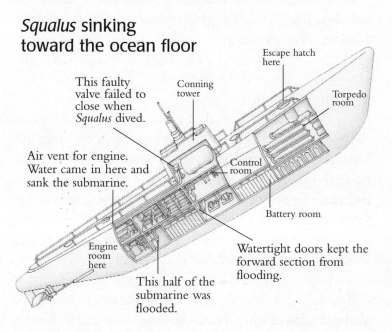

Escape hatch here

This faulty valve failed to close when *Squalus* dived.

Conning tower

Torpedo room

Air vent for engine. Water came in here and sank the submarine.

Control room

Battery room

Engine room here

Watertight doors kept the forward section from flooding.

This half of the submarine was flooded.

Four minutes passed before *Squalus* hit the bottom with a jarring thud. But the hull held firm. This much they had survived. When the ship had settled, several flashlights were brought out, and small cones of light pierced the pitch dark. Naquin and Doyle began to take stock of the situation. Water had entered via an open air vent to the engine room. Their "Christmas tree" had indicated that all vents were closed to the sea, so a fault must have developed in both the vent's closing mechanism, and the indicator light.

That much was obvious. But who of the crew was still left alive? In the ghostly glow of a flashlight, Charles Kuney, who manned the control room intercom, tried to contact all sections of the submarine. His calls to the rear of the ship met with an ominous silence.

It gradually became clear that all compartments behind the control room were now flooded, and the 26 men normally stationed in the aft battery room and both engine rooms must have been trapped and drowned. In the forward section, 33 men remained alive. Some were bruised and bleeding, but none were seriously injured.

Things could be worse, thought Naquin to himself. But one thought was bothering him immensely. He knew the only thing they could do was wait to be rescued. But the control room depth gauge showed that they were 73m (240ft) below the surface. No submarine crew had ever before been rescued from this far beneath the sea.

Naquin tried to dismiss such thoughts, and immediately instructed his crew to release emergency flares, which floated to the surface and then launched themselves into the air. A marker buoy was also sent up from the submarine, with a telephone link to enable any rescuers to communicate with the crew. It carried a sign saying:

"Submarine sunk here.

Telephone inside."

If the marker buoy or flares were not spotted, the navy authorities would soon know something was wrong. *Squalus* was due to report back to base at her next scheduled call in at 9:40 that morning.

The most immediate problem the crew faced was suffocation. Not only did they need a supply of air to breathe, but there was also the danger of asphyxiation by poisonous carbon dioxide gas, which each man produced with every exhaled breath.

The ship's batteries presented another lethal danger. Chemicals inside them could react with sea water to produce deadly chlorine gas, and water inside the hull was slowly rising all the time.

To conserve their air supply, Naquin ordered his men to remain as still and as quiet as possible, with no talking or moving around unless absolutely necessary. Soda lime, a powder which absorbs carbon dioxide, was sprinkled around the ship. All hands were issued with a "Momsen Lung". This was a crude form of aqualung, shaped like a rubber hot-water bottle attached to a breathing mask. It was designed to give a sailor enough air to breathe while he tried to swim

13

from a submarine escape hatch up to the surface. *Squalus* was almost certainly too deep for such a device to be effective, but the "Lungs" could be used by the crew for a refreshing blast of fresh air, when the air inside the hull became too foul to breathe.

In the dim haze of the emergency lights that now lit the submarine's interior, the surviving members of the crew curled up in corners. There was nothing to do now but wait.

❖

Back at Portsmouth, the *Squalus*'s failure to contact her home base had been noted, and a rescue operation was now being mounted. By 1:00 that afternoon, a team of divers – including underwater rescue expert Charles "Swede" Momsen, inventor of the Momsen Lung – had been summoned from Washington, and were flying in by seaplane. *Squalus*'s sister ship, *Sculpin*, and several tugs were dispatched to her last reported position to assist in any rescue.

In New London, 320km (200 miles) south of Portsmouth, the US Navy rescue vessel *Falcon* also set sail to join them. *Falcon* carried a McCann Rescue Chamber – a newly invented diving bell based on an idea of Momsen's. But it had never been used in a real-life rescue before, and training exercises had been in much shallower water.

Aboard the *Squalus*, at noon, a meal of canned fruit was handed out. Sugar in the food would warm the chilly crew. Then soon after lunch something else happened to lift their spirits – they heard the dull drubbing of propeller blades above the ship. Five hours after their catastrophic dive, *Sculpin* had arrived. The surface submarine swiftly located the marker buoy sent up earlier that day, and her captain quickly made contact with Naquin via the telephone in the buoy.

But no sooner had Naquin reeled off the depth and location of his sunken submarine than the telephone line snapped, cutting *Squalus* off from the outside world. It was 7:30 that evening before rescuers located her again, after the tug *Penacook* had trawled for four hours and finally hooked an anchor onto a railing on *Squalus*'s deck.

Inside the sunken submarine the temperature was now falling rapidly to that of the sea outside – a near freezing 4°C (39°F). Dank, dripping condensation filled the already water-logged interior, and flood water inside the hull was still slowly rising. Naquin ordered a meal of beans, tomatoes and fruit to be given out. Now it was much colder, he also had blankets distributed to his weary crew. The stale air had made them drowsy and, despite their fear and the cold, many whiled away the waiting hours in an uneasy sleep.

On the surface another tug, *Wandank*, had arrived, and disturbed the dozing crew with the noise of an onboard oscillator. This device sent a high-pitched tone underwater and could be used to transmit Morse code – a form of signalling in which a series of short or longer bleeps stands for each letter of the alphabet.

When he heard the piercing ping of the oscillator, Naquin immediately ordered two of his men to the conning tower to reply. Using a small sledgehammer, they hammered out a response on the thin metal cover of the tower. Slowly and carefully, they passed on the news that only 33 of the submarine's crew remained alive.

It was not until 4:20 the next morning that *Falcon* and its rescue chamber arrived. Aboard the ship was Allen McCann, the chamber's chief designer, who was anxious to know how his invention would work at such a depth. But Momsen, who was in overall charge of the rescue operation, was still unsure of what to do. Maybe water could be pumped out of the flooded rear section, and the submarine would rise to the surface?

But no one on the surface knew why *Squalus* had sunk, so this idea was rejected. Momsen also wondered whether the men could use his "Momsen

Lungs" to escape. But the submarine was too deep to be sure they had enough air to reach the top. Untried though it was, the McCann Rescue Chamber looked like the best option available.

So, by 9:30 that morning, *Falcon* had anchored herself directly above *Squalus*, and a diver was lowered down into the ocean to attach a thick guide cable to the submarine's escape hatch. The small flotilla of rescue ships on the surface had now been joined by another boat full of journalists, who had made a choppy 15-hour journey out to the scene of the accident.

The diver succeeded in placing the cable on *Squalus*, and crew in the hull cheered when they heard his footsteps on the deck. Everything was now in place, and the McCann's Rescue Chamber was about to be used for its first real rescue. Momsen picked his two best divers to go down with it. Then the chamber was carefully winched over the side of *Falcon*.

The journey from the surface down to the stricken submarine took 15 minutes. Eventually, the chamber made contact with *Squalus*'s bow, and then steel bolts anchored it in position over the escape hatch. As water drained away, a sailor in *Squalus* rapidly began to turn the wheel that secured the hatch in place.

Lowering the Rescue Chamber

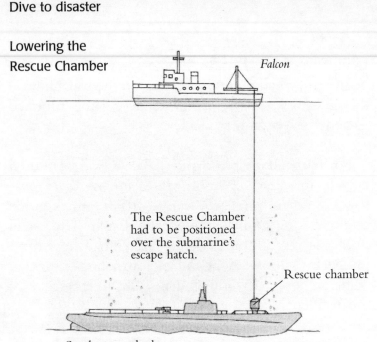

Falcon

The Rescue Chamber had to be positioned over the submarine's escape hatch.

Rescue chamber

Squalus on seabed

It soon swung open and a blast of foul and freezing air rushed into the chamber. The men inside looked down the hatch to see a collection of dull, drawn faces looking up at them. The divers had expected at least a cheer or welcome, and were stunned by the silence that greeted them. One of them, rather lost for words, said at last, "Well, we're here!"

Perhaps the survivors on the *Squalus* did not realize that the arrival of the chamber meant that their lives had been saved? Perhaps they suspected that there was still a great deal of danger to endure before they would return safely to the surface?

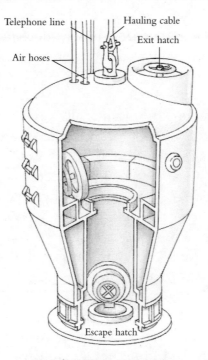

Telephone line

Hauling cable

Exit hatch

Air hoses

Escape hatch

McCann Rescue Chamber

As soon as the hatch opened, the divers in the chamber began to pass down soup, coffee and sandwiches. Then clean air was pumped down from the surface, filling the *Squalus* with wonderful, fresh, life-giving oxygen.

After an hour, it was time to return to the top. Seven men climbed into the chamber. After a slow ascent, it broke surface and was hauled aboard the *Falcon*. Momsen and McCann were delighted. Their invention had worked. They could see no reason why the remaining 26 men on board the *Squalus* should not be rescued, and so the chamber was readied for another dive.

But inside the submarine all was far from well. Thick, choking clouds of chlorine gas were rising from batteries contaminated by sea water. As soon as he realized the danger, Naquin acted quickly. Before anyone could be poisoned by the gas, he led his remaining crew through to the forward torpedo room. The bulkhead door to the battery room was then sealed, to prevent any more of the gas from reaching them.

Now the survivors were crammed into an even smaller space. There was nothing to do but huddle down, as they had done before, and wait for rescue. As they waited, Naquin reflected that his crew had acted with great courage. Despite their terrible predicament, and the death of half their shipmates, no one had panicked, or disobeyed orders.

On the surface, the diving chamber was readied for its next descent. But, as soon as it was lowered into the water, the cable jammed and the chamber had to be hoisted up to the surface again. This time, the descent was made without further problems, and nine men were rescued. Another trip followed without incident, and now only eight men remained inside the stricken submarine.

By the time the divers were ready for their final descent, dusk had fallen over the ocean, and searchlights lit the chamber as it entered the water. Once again the docking with *Squalus* went smoothly, and the final eight men, including Naquin and Doyle, climbed aboard. They could hardly believe their lives were to be spared from the disaster that had overtaken their submarine. But the sea was reluctant to give up its victims and the next three hours would be quietly terrifying.

❖

The ascent began at 8:40pm. But, halfway up, the cable hauling the chamber to the surface jammed. The two divers operating it hit the motor with their fists, then kicked it in a rage. Nothing moved. There was only one thing left to do – the chamber would have to return to the submarine, and a diver would have to be sent down to free the cable.

The 10 men waited patiently. At least there was light and air in the chamber, and they were in radio contact with the surface. But everyone knew how dangerous their situation was. Who could say for sure they would not be trapped here, as they had been aboard the *Squalus*?

Eventually, a tapping on the side of the chamber told them a diver had arrived. He quickly freed the jammed reel, and the chamber began to climb up to the *Falcon* at a steady 1.5m (5ft) a minute.

But there was more trouble in store. On the surface, in the stark light of the searchlights, men on board the *Falcon* noticed strands in the cable had begun to snap and unravel. These strands must have been damaged when the cable had jammed.

Momsen again ordered the chamber to return to the bottom of the ocean. The men inside could not believe how fate was taunting them. Again, they sat through another slow descent until a dull clang told them they had reached the submarine. Once again they endured another terrible wait until the chamber moved again. Staring down at the hatch at the bottom of the chamber Naquin could imagine his dead crew members floating in the hull, silently beckoning him to join them.

On board the *Falcon* there was feverish activity. Another diver was sent down to fasten a new cable to the chamber, but he was swiftly overcome with exhaustion and had to be pulled back to the surface. Yet another diver entered the chilly water and descended to the sea bottom, but he too failed to attach the new cable. Divers in the 1930s wore heavy, clumsy outfits and needed to be exceptionally strong. Working in deep water was highly dangerous, and a diver could stay underwater for only a few minutes at a time. At night, such underwater work was even more difficult.

Momson was defeated. There was nothing left to do but haul the chamber to the surface with its fraying cable. Fearful that the steam pulley which usually hauled it in would pull too hard and snap the cable, Momsen and McCann decided their men would have to pull the chamber up by hand.

So, in a freezing wind, and after an exhausting day, a team of men began the laborious task of dragging the chamber to the surface, hauling and relaxing the cable with the swell of the sea.

After 10 minutes, the threadbare section of cable emerged from the sea. Momsen could see that it was as thin as a piece of string. Watching with wide-eyed trepidation, he found himself bathed in sweat, despite the cold.

With incredible delicacy, a clamp was attached to the cable below the break. Once this was done, the crew on the *Falcon* knew they had saved the men in the chamber. If the cable broke now, they had another one attached to it, to reel it in.

The chamber was eventually winched aboard at 12:38am, and the final survivors of *Squalus* staggered out on to the deck of the *Falcon*. After their 40-hour ordeal, the chill night air and stinging sea spray had never felt so wonderful.

After the ordeal

Squalus was salvaged (brought back from the sea bottom) six months after its disastrous dive. Pumped full of air, it rose to the surface with such force that its bow shot 9m (30ft) out of the water. When shown a photograph of this, American president Franklin Roosevelt joked that it looked like a sailfish leaping out of the water. Navies traditionally rename all salvaged ships, so *Squalus* became known as *Sailfish*.

Although all its electronic equipment was ruined by sea water and had to be replaced, much of the submarine was undamaged. With four of the original *Squalus* crew on board, *Sailfish* went on to fight in World War Two against the Japanese in the Pacific. *Sailfish* survived the war, and was then broken up for scrap. On Veteran's Day 1946, sections of *Sailfish*, including the bridge, conning tower and part of the deck, were unveiled as a memorial in Portsmouth Harbor, to those who had died in the submarine service. This memorial can still be seen today.

Sculpin, which had helped in the rescue operation, was less lucky in the war. In November 1943 she was sunk by Japanese Navy ships, and 21 of the crew were taken prisoner. They were placed on board a Japanese aircraft carrier, *Chuyo*, which was attacked and sunk a month later by *Sailfish*. Only one of *Sculpin*'s crew survived.

Hindenburg's hydrogen inferno

Perhaps the *Hindenburg* was the most amazing flying machine ever built. Its size alone was extraordinary. At 245m (804ft) long, it was as big as an ocean liner – a mere 23m (78ft) shorter than the Titanic.

Most of the airship was made up of 16 huge bags (called cells) of hydrogen gas. This was what lifted the craft into the sky, as hydrogen is lighter than air. Once airborne, the airship was driven along at 125kmph (78mph) by four powerful 1,100 horsepower diesel engines.

The skin of the *Hindenburg* was painted a silky, elegant grey, but on its tail were two black and red swastikas – the symbol of Germany's ruling Nazi party. Partly built with the help of state aid from the Nazis, right from the start of its life in 1936 the *Hindenburg* was seen as a symbol of German might and prestige. No sooner had it made its first few test flights than Nazi propaganda minister Joseph Goebbels ordered it to fly over every German city with a population larger than 100,000. It would arrive blaring patriotic music from loudspeakers and dropping Nazi Party propaganda leaflets on the astounded citizens below.

Barely two months after its maiden voyage, the *Hindenburg* began to fly across the Atlantic, taking passengers between Frankfurt, Germany and Lakehurst, New Jersey, an airport just outside New York City. The service was a fantastic success, despite the fact that the cost – $810 there and back – was astronomical. (In 1936 this would have been enough money to buy a new family car.)

Expensive it may have been, but the rich of Europe and America flocked to use the service. At the time, it was the only airborne crossing of the Atlantic (aircraft flights did not begin until 1939), and the journey could be done in a breathtaking two and a half days. In the 1930s the quickest transatlantic crossing by sea was at least five days.

The opulent interior of the *Hindenburg* was designed to make any passenger feel that their money was being well spent. Behind the control gondola below the nose were two decks fitted into the vast steel frame structure of the airship. On the upper deck was the passenger accommodation. Passengers slept in 25 cabins, each lined with pearly-grey linen and furnished with two bunk-style berths and hot and cold running water.

Inside the *Hindenburg*

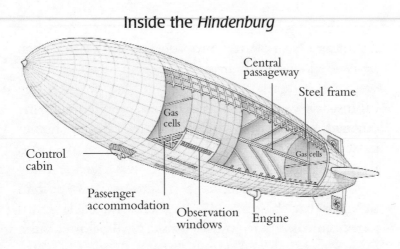

As with any exclusive hotel, shoes could be left outside the doors to be cleaned overnight by staff. There was a promenade and lounge each side of the craft, with huge observation windows which could be opened. Inside the lounge were lightweight but elegant tables and chairs, and even a grand piano made of ultralight metal covered in yellow pigskin. The dining room offered such German culinary delights as Bavarian-style fattened duckling and roast gosling, which could be washed down with the best available German wines.

The lower deck contained the crew's quarters and galley (kitchen) which used electric stoves. There was also a passenger bar with a smoking room, which contained one electric lighter. Connected to the rest of the airship via an airlock, it was designed to allow passengers to drink and smoke without any danger of igniting the hydrogen gas which kept the *Hindenburg* airborne. Everything was designed to be both lightweight and luxurious, although some corners were cut in order to keep down the weight. The cabins, for example, were separated only by foam-covered fabric, and there was only one shower between 50 or so passengers.

The first year's transatlantic service in 1936 had been a great success, and each of the *Hindenburg*'s 10 flights had been fully booked. Airships were notoriously vulnerable to bad weather, so the service only ran in the spring and summer months, and began again the following year in May.

The first Atlantic crossing of 1937 began on the evening of May 3, at Rhein-Main World Airport, Frankfurt. Aboard were 42 passengers and 55 members of the crew. This first flight was not a sell-out, but the Deutsche Zeppelin-Reederei company that operated the *Hindenburg* was confident their service would still bring in a profitable supply of rich and famous passengers throughout the summer.

With all his passengers and luggage aboard, Captain Max Pruss ordered: "*Schiff hoch!*" ("Up Ship!") and the ground crew released the mooring ropes that kept the *Hindenburg* anchored to the ground. To mark the first flight of the year, a brass band in blue and yellow uniforms stood on the runway playing the German national anthem, and other patriotic tunes.

Free to float upward, the airship's seven million cubic feet of hydrogen gas lifted the craft into the air. It rose so gently the passengers on board only realized they were taking off because the waving figures on the ground were gradually getting smaller. One journalist who had taken an earlier flight was so impressed by the smoothness of the airship's flight, he wrote: "You feel as though you were carried in the arms of angels". Sometimes passengers who boarded the evening flight and retired to their cabins did not even realize the airship had taken off. With good reason, the Zeppelin company boasted that no passenger had ever suffered from air sickness.

When the airship reached 90m (300ft), huge wooden propellers began to turn on the four diesel engines, drowning out the band below. With a thunderous drone the *Hindenburg* vanished into the night. On that evening in May the weather was perfect, and passengers spent a thrilling hour before supper watching the gleaming beacons of small towns and huge pools of city lights roll leisurely past beneath them.

Captain Max Pruss sat confidently in the forward control gondola. A veteran World War One zeppelin commander, he had spent many years flying these huge airships. Among his responsibilities was ensuring the *Hindenburg* remained stable in its flight. A roll of more than two degrees from the horizontal could send wine bottles crashing from tables and play havoc with food preparation in the galley.

With Pruss in the dimly lit cabin was Ernst Lehmann, director of the Zeppelin company. Both men had every faith in their magnificent craft, but were all too well aware that the safety record of huge airships over the previous few years had been unsettling. In 1930, Britain's R101 had crashed in flames, and almost all on board had been killed. The USA had had no more success mastering these aerial giants. Two similarly huge craft had both crashed within two years of their maiden flights.

Still, despite the problems other nations faced, Germany had built themselves an enviable reputation as the only country capable of flying airships without disaster. For six years now, there had been a successful passenger service. Germany had been the first to invent and make widespread use of these craft, so perhaps their experience gave them the edge.

But even the *Hindenburg* had potentially fatal flaws, not least the lighter-than-air gas that German airships used to lift themselves into the sky. Hydrogen is the same element that burns so fiercely on the Sun. If a gas cell leaked, a mere spark could cause an inferno.

31

The *Hindenburg* flew confidently on, over the Atlantic. When the airship reached Newfoundland, Pruss took her down low to give his passengers a closer look at the beautiful icebergs lining their way.

The flight reached New York on May 6 – three days after leaving Frankfurt. Strong winds had delayed their arrival time at Lakehurst by several hours. Crossing over Manhattan, the *Hindenburg* flew so low over the Empire State Building that passengers could clearly see photographers on top of the skyscraper snapping away.

It was early afternoon when the *Hindenburg* approached Lakehurst Airfield. But storms were brewing, and Captain Pruss decided that the winds were too strong and that the *Hindenburg* should wait a while before she landed. Below, family and friends who had turned up to meet passengers at Lakehurst at the scheduled arrival time of 6:00am, faced an even more frustrating wait.

Among them were scores of newspaper, newsreel and radio journalists, eager to record the arrival of this modern-day wonder. The *Hindenburg* was still a tremendous novelty, and a large crowd of onlookers had gathered to watch her land.

Eventually the decision was made to bring the *Hindenburg* in. At 5:00pm a siren at the airfield sounded, to summon the 92 navy and 139 civilian airfield personnel needed to handle the mooring lines that would hold the *Hindenburg* to the ground. At 7:10pm the airship began its final descent. Aboard, the passengers gathered with their luggage in the ship's lounge, ready to disembark down the airship's main stairway.

❖

Watching the scene was radio reporter Herb Morrison, broadcasting live for a Chicago radio station. His report began peacefully enough. As the airship loomed out of the evening sky and drifted down to her mooring mast, he told his listeners:

"Here it comes, ladies and gentlemen, and what a sight it is. . . a thrilling one, a magnificent sight. The mighty diesel engines roar."

But death was waiting for the *Hindenburg* at Lakehurst. At 7:25pm, just forward of the mighty tail fins, two crewmen inside the ship noticed a sight that turned their blood to ice. Lurking in the middle of the number four gas cell was a bright blue and yellow ball of curling fire.

On the ground, observers could see a faint pink glow inside the ship, which gave it a curiously transparent quality. One witness likened it to a Japanese lantern. Then, within a second, the entire cell exploded with a muffled WHUUMP, and fierce flames burst out of the silver canvas covering. A huge, orange fireball erupted into a gigantic mushroom of smoke and flames, and began to devour the still airborne vessel.

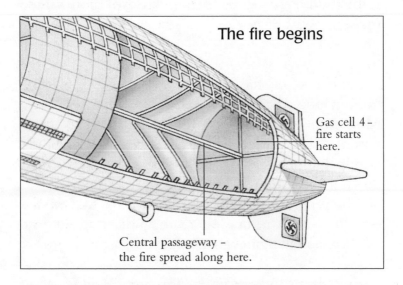

The fire begins

Gas cell 4 – fire starts here.

Central passageway – the fire spread along here.

Herb Morrison watched aghast, his voice turning from awed appreciation to hysteria.

"It's burst into flame! Get out of the way! Get out of the way, please!" he begged the aircrew on the ground. "This is terrible. This is one of the worst catastrophes in the world! The flames are 500 feet into the sky."

Most of the passengers and crew were in the front section of the *Hindenburg*. Their first inkling of the disaster was seeing figures below scatter in panic over the wet ground, which had suddenly taken on a garish red glow. Within seconds the ship was lurching wildly, and flames engulfed the passenger decks.

In the control cabin, the initial explosion was so muffled one officer just thought a landing rope had broken. But then frenzied shouts of "FIRE" alerted the crew to the true situation. As hydrogen gas at the rear of the *Hindenburg* burned away, the airship sank, bottom down. As the stern fell, the bow rose, and passengers preparing to jump from the open observation windows saw the ground, and their hopes of survival, reel rapidly away from them.

The sharp angle of the *Hindenburg* turned the central passageway that ran from its tip to its tail into a chimney, and a huge tongue of flame shot out from its nose − "like fire from a volcano," said one witness. Crewmen in the forward section clung hopelessly to metal girders but, scorched by the heat, they lost their grip and fell into the swirling inferno below. But as the fire from the rear spread throughout the body of the *Hindenburg*, and gas burned off more evenly, the ship began to level off, and settled on the ground with a ghastly hiss.

Herb Morrison could not bear to watch.
"Oh, the humanity! Those passengers. I can't talk, ladies and gentlemen. . . Honest, it is a mass of

smoking wreckage. . . I am going to step inside where I can't see it. Listen folks, I am going to have to stop for a minute because I have lost my voice."

❖

Then, to the amazement of onlookers, people began to stumble and crawl from the raging conflagration. With extraordinary bravery, ground crew, who seconds before had been running for their lives, turned around and plunged into the burning wreck, "like dogs after rabbits," said one eyewitness.

Those who survived generally owed their lives to where they were on the ship. The crewmen in the tail, who had seen the fire start, dashed to safety when the stern hit the ground. Flames and heat always rise upward, so those under the explosion were in the best position to make a successful escape.

Some passengers used their wits to save themselves. One, a professional acrobat, hung from a window sill as the ship rose and fell, only jumping when he knew he could survive the fall. Another, finding himself lying on the ground surrounded by burning rubble, burrowed under the wet sand to safety.

Others were just lucky. One dazed, elderly woman simply walked down the ship's retractable steps, which had been broken open by the violent landing. One crew member survived the flames when a water tank burst open above him, momentarily dousing a clear path away from the blaze.

One passenger, Leonhard Adelt, realized the airship was ablaze when it was 37m (120ft) from the ground. As he contemplated jumping, the ship suddenly hit the ground with a tremendous impact which threw him and his wife against the floor. Tables and chairs piled up and blocked their exit, so they leapt 6m (20ft) from the open window onto the soft sand below. Then everything went black as the airship crashed down on top of them.

Surrounded by burning oily clouds, they clawed through the white-hot metal struts and wires. Too numb with shock to feel pain, they struggled to find a route to safety. Adelt remembered, "It was like a dream. Our bodies had no weight. They floated like stars through space."

Another passenger on the *Hindenburg*, Margaret Mather, remembered that when the ship stood sharply on its stern, she was thrown into a corner and several other people landed on top of her. Then flames, "bright red and very beautiful," blew into the passenger area. Mather watched others jump from the windows, but she was too stunned to move, imagining she was in "a medieval picture of an inferno". Then a loud cry brought her quickly to her senses. "Aren't you coming?" shouted one of the ground crew who had dived into the flames, and out she ran.

❖

In the control cabin beneath the ship, 12 officers and men were the last to leave. As white-hot metal crashed around them, they forged a path through the flames. Captain Pruss attempted to rescue a trapped crewman, and burned his face badly. Ernst Lehmann had more severe injuries. He emerged from the wreckage a human torch. Onlookers beat the flames from his burning clothes as he mumbled, "I don't understand it." The future of his company had gone up in smoke. He died early the next morning.

The whole airship had been engulfed by fire in a mere 32 seconds. Because the *Hindenburg* was a world-famous phenomenon, and because journalists had been present at Lakehurst in such great numbers, pictures and stories of the catastrophe quickly flashed around the world. People everywhere were stunned by the tragedy, much as they had been by the sinking of the Titanic, 25 years earlier.

The flames died down leaving only a burning hot skeleton of twisted metal. Altogether 35 people on board the *Hindenburg* died. One man on the ground was also killed. But perhaps the most extraordinary aspect of the disaster was that 62 passengers and crew were able to walk out of the wreckage and live to tell the tale.

After the ordeal

Herb Morrison's radio report had been recorded, and was broadcast all around the world. His horrified account can still be heard today whenever newsreel footage of the disaster is shown in television documentaries.

In Germany, members of the ruling Nazi party saw the *Hindenburg* as a symbol of the power and prestige of the Third Reich. They were quick to blame the disaster on sabotage, but could produce no serious evidence to back this up. A board of inquiry set up to investigate the fire concluded it was caused by a hydrogen gas leak ignited by a spark of static electricity.

Hugo Eckener, chairman of the Zeppelin company, described the airship's fire as "the hopeless end of a great dream". The notion of huge airships carrying passengers across the ocean died in the flames at Lakehurst. To this day, airships remain an airborne gimmick, suitable mainly for advertising slogans.

The cause of the fire is still controversial. Some scientists are convinced that it was not hydrogen that caught fire, but the fabric skin of the *Hindenburg*. There are several compelling reasons why this might be the case. Hydrogen burns with a blue or neutral flame, whereas witnesses compared the *Hindenburg* fire with "a fireworks display", with bright red and orange flames. The *Hindenburg* did not drop to the ground immediately, which also suggests that it was something else burning, rather than hydrogen.

The skin of the *Hindenburg* was coated with a mixture of ground metals and other chemicals, to ensure it was taut and durable. This chemical combination was highly inflammable, and has recently been described by one scientist as "a respectable rocket propellant".

Despite their insistence that sabotage was the cause of the disaster, the Nazis quietly changed the skin coating of the *Graf Zeppelin*, the sister ship of the *Hindenburg*, to a less combustible mixture. This airship, which was also lifted into the air by hydrogen gas, went on to fly over a million miles without incident.

Some aeronautical scientists think that the use of hydrogen, both as a fuel and as a way of lifting aircraft, has been unfairly overlooked in the development of aerial transportation because of the

Hindenburg disaster. They point out that hydrogen is no more inflammable and dangerous than petrol (gasoline) which is used all the time.

Captain Bligh's boatload of trouble

William Bligh, captain of Royal Navy vessel *Bounty*, began the morning of April 28, 1789, tied to a mast on the deck of his ship. He was surrounded by his mutinous crew, who even now were wondering whether or not to kill him.

The leader of the mutineers was Bligh's own second in command, Fletcher Christian. The two men had once been close friends and perhaps it was this that had saved Bligh's life. Christian had argued fiercely with his fellow mutineers to stop them from killing their hated captain on the spot.

The man tied to the mast was a curious mixture of qualities. He was honest, and had a strong sense of duty, but he also had an arrogant manner and terrible temper. He often subjected the ship's officers, especially Christian, to public and withering contempt.

The mutiny had been a long time coming, and a more sensitive man than Bligh would have taken steps to avoid it. The *Bounty* was on an around-the-world trip to deliver breadfruit plants from the Pacific to slave plantations in the West Indies, where slave owners thought it would provide cheap food for their slaves. After a harsh and difficult voyage the *Bounty* had recently spent a lengthy stopover in Tahiti. Here the crew had enjoyed the beautiful island, and the company of its friendly inhabitants.

They found it difficult to adjust to life back at sea. Bligh, in turn, felt his crew were slacking, and that harsh discipline was called for to lick them back into shape. In the days before the mutiny his unthinking persecution of Christian had intensified, and he continued to humiliate him in front of the crew. Christian resented this intensely, and his loyalty to Bligh withered away. The Captain's bullying manner also lost him the respect of the crew he once addressed as "a parcel of lubberly rascals".

Now, Christian and the mutineers intended to sail back to Tahiti and the life they had enjoyed there, but first there were two serious problems to resolve. Firstly, what would they do with Captain Bligh? Secondly, not all the crew had mutinied – 18 men had remained loyal to their captain, and they were currently under guard, elsewhere on the ship.

Despite all the resentment he felt toward him, Christian could not bring himself to kill Bligh.

Neither could he kill those of the crew still loyal to their captain. These were fellow shipmates for whom he bore no ill-will at all. So a compromise was reached. Bligh, and all those loyal to him, would be placed in a small boat loaded with supplies, and set adrift.

So, on that April morning, Bligh and 18 of his crew were ushered off the *Bounty* at bayonet point and crammed into the ship's launch, so tightly there was no room to lie down. On the boat were five days' food and drink, and a handful of navigation instruments.

The sailors on the launch pulled away from the *Bounty*, with the catcalls and jeers of the mutineers ringing in their ears. Ahead lay a very uncertain future. Christian had given them a fighting chance, at least, although he had also put their lives in very grave danger.

❖

Gradually the *Bounty* grew smaller and smaller, until it became a small speck and drifted over the horizon. Aboard the tiny launch Bligh and his loyal crew felt terribly alone in the huge ocean. Their boat had oars and sails, but it was designed for short journeys between ship and shore, and was in no way suitable for the kind of voyage they would have to undertake in order to survive. For now, the weather was calm, but these were often stormy seas.

Overcrowding on the boat also made a bad situation worse. Bligh's men were cold, wet and very hungry, they could not sleep and were constantly having to bail out water in order to keep the launch afloat. As well as this, some of the men felt deep resentment towards Bligh, and thought he was to blame for the mutiny. For many on the boat, their loyalty to him was based not on respect but fear of the law. They knew that being part of the mutiny meant they could never return home. At best they would face a lifetime in exile, and at worst a military execution in the form of slow strangulation at the end of a rope and yard-arm.

Bligh knew, more than any of them, the dangers ahead. He had sailed these waters some years previously with Captain Cook, the famous Pacific explorer, who had been killed by hostile islanders. He also knew that their nearest safe haven was a Dutch trading colony at Kupang, on the island of Timor. Here they could rejoin a British ship and make their way home. But Timor was 6,300km (3,900 miles) away. A journey like that could take 50 days.

Bligh decided their first priority would be to find food for the journey, so he directed the launch toward Tofua Island, which the *Bounty* had passed on the night before the mutiny. He knew nothing of the islanders there, and had to trust to luck that they would be friendly.

The launch landed on a sandy cove on the island. The men waded ashore, grateful to be away from their cramped little boat. They rested as best they could, and looked for food, but all they could find was a handful of coconuts. On the next day, islanders came to visit them. At first these people were friendly, and traded food for the men's uniform buttons and beads. But when they realized Bligh's crew were castaways, and not a party from an armed ship, their attitude changed, and they became more aggressive.

Bligh realized too late that a kind of hostile standoff had developed. He and his men needed to leave the island as soon as possible, but they all knew their leaving might provoke an all-out attack. The longer they stayed, the worse the situation became. More islanders were arriving at the beach. They gathered together in groups and began to knock stones together in a sinister, intimidating manner. Bligh had seen islanders behave like this shortly before Captain Cook had been killed.

Beckoning his crew to gather around, Bligh spoke to them in a low voice.

"I fear these savages mean to kill us," he told them

bluntly, "and will do so as soon as we intend to leave. I propose that we wait until nightfall, and slowly fill our boat. Then we will tell our friends here we shall sleep at sea and trade with them again in the morning."

Bligh's crew were all too aware of the danger they were in, and looked to their captain to save them. All agreed that this was the best thing to do.

As dusk fell over the beach, the launch was duly loaded. But, as the men inched toward their boat, the islanders all stood up and again began to knock stones together. When Bligh's men reached the water's edge the stones rained down on them, and the islanders charged toward them.

The ship's quartermaster, John Norton, was closest to the shore, and he bravely turned to face their attackers. He was immediately struck down and savagely clubbed to death, but his great courage saved his crewmates. The rest of them reached the launch, and cast off to sea. As the islanders followed through the shallow surf, Bligh and others distracted them by throwing clothes overboard. This ruse worked successfully. The islanders stopped to pick the clothes up, and the boat sailed out of reach to the safety of the open sea.

Bruised and terrified by their encounter, the crew sailed on in grim silence. They passed other lush, green islands along their route back to Timor, but no one dared even suggest they land there.

The food on board the launch was pitifully inadequate for such a long journey. There were a few coconuts brought from the Tofuans, a supply of ship's biscuits, which were rapidly going rotten, a few pieces of salted pork, 12 bottles of rum, and several barrels of fresh water. Bligh realized that to have any chance of survival they would have to ration their provisions very carefully.

He stood on the stern of the launch and addressed his weary crew.

"God willing, if we complete our journey successfully, we shall be at sea at least 50 days. Our provisions must last this amount of time. We have but a miserable ration, and I can give each man here no more than one ounce of biscuit, and one quarter pint of water a day. I ask each of you to swear before the others that he will accept the ration I give him, and not ask for more."

Something in Bligh's manner must have reassured the crew. They all agreed that this is what they would do, and sailed away from Tofua in good spirits. Two days passed and the launch made good progress, but on the third morning away from Tofua, the sun rose red and fiery – a sure sign that a storm would soon be upon them. But that morning brought more ill luck. As they passed the island of Waia, two large sailing canoes set out after them, causing great alarm in the launch. The men were sure that if the canoes caught up with them, they would be killed and eaten.

Bligh took firm command, ordering six of his strongest men to the oars, and they rowed for their very lives. For three terrible hours the canoes gave chase, only to abandon their quarry in the early afternoon. But no sooner had the crew recovered from that harrowing chase, than the weather came to torment them. The wind began to howl and torrential rain tore into the fragile boat.

That night was the worst one yet. Bligh noted in his log: "We bore away across the sea where the navigation is but little known (and) not a star could be seen to steer by." Everyone was too cold and miserable to sleep, and when dawn finally came the storm showed no sign at all of receding. But it was now that Bligh showed the kind of leadership and humanity that would have saved him from his mutiny had he the sense to realize it before. He cheerfully instructed his crew to remove their clammy, sodden clothes and dip them in the sea, which was warmer than the rain. When they had done this, he gave each man a spoonful of rum, which also warmed them up.

Bligh knew that sailors cast away in open boats often become listless and apathetic. They curl up motionless, as static as their changeless circumstances. He was determined to prevent this from happening, and knew the only way to survive would be to keep the crew alert and in good spirits. To do this he divided the men into two groups. While one group sailed the boat, the others lay in the bottom and rested. The two groups switched every four hours. This routine gave shape to what would have been an otherwise endless, shapeless day.

To fill the long hours Bligh turned the highlight of each day – the handing out of rations at 8:00 in the morning, noon and sunset – into a lengthy ritual. The daily amount for each man was weighed out on a scale made from two coconut halves. A couple of pistol bullets served as weights and the whole process of preparing each portion kept the entire crew entranced.

Biscuits were always on the menu, but Bligh kept his small supply of salted pork as an occasional surprise, delighting the boat by handing out tiny strips. Bligh invited his men to make their paltry rations last as long as any ordinary meal. He always broke his food into tiny morsels, and ate it very slowly.

Occasionally someone on the boat caught a seabird that was unlucky enough to land on the side of the boat. This was swiftly killed and then shared out in a naval custom called "Who shall have this?" Firstly, the bird was cut into small sections. Then, one man pointed to a piece and called out, "Who shall have this?" Another man, who had his back to them all, called out a name at random, and the piece went to that man. In this way arguments about who ate which part of the bird were avoided. In his log, Bligh wryly noted the "great amusement" in the boat, when he was given such unappetizing parts as the beak or feet to eat.

Between meals, Bligh would often entertain his men with stories about earlier voyages, and encourage them to share their own adventures. He was a brilliant navigator and seaman, and drew maps to show them where they were going, and how far they had gone. Each night he led his crew in pitiful prayers, saying, "Bless our miserable morsel of bread, and may it be sufficient for our undertaking."

When spirits sagged he would try to lift them with cheerful sailors' songs. He also had the shrewd idea of getting the crew to sew together a patchwork Union Jack flag from bundles of signal flags that had been thrown into the boat when they had left the *Bounty*. Bligh told them they would use this flag to identify themselves when they sailed into Kupang port, in Timor. But making the flag also kept the men occupied, and was a symbol of hope for the end of their ordeal.

For 15 days the tiny boat pushed on through an unbroken spell of bad weather, and the men were constantly drenched and freezing. In his log book, which Bligh diligently continued to fill in, he recorded:

"We were so covered with rain and salt we could scarcely see. Our appearances were horrible. I could look no way, but I caught the eye of someone in distress. Extreme hunger was now too evident. The little sleep we got was in the midst of water, and we constantly awoke with cramps and pains in our bones."

Worse was to come. 21 days into the voyage, Bligh realized their biscuits were not going to last. The ration would have to be cut from three to two portions a day. Although the men took the news without protest, the decision, he wrote in his log, was like robbing them of life.

Then, at last, on May 24 he was able to write: "For the first time, during the last fifteen days, we experienced comfort and warmth from the sun." They sailed on for another week, and although Bligh's well thought out routine kept them going, the crew were visibly fading before his eyes. Then, nearly a month into the journey, they began to notice signs of land. Not island land, which they had avoided for fear of their lives, but the huge continent of Australia, then known as New Holland.

At first they saw a broken branch float by. Then many birds began to wheel around the launch. Best of all, there were clouds, which always form around the coast, which could be constantly seen on the western horizon. When the sound of the sea roaring against rocks was carried toward them by the wind, the men knew they would soon be standing on solid ground.

❖

On May 28, their small boat passed carefully through the Great Barrier Reef, just off the Australian coast. The continent was still almost entirely unknown and almost certainly hostile territory. At the time, there was only one European settlement there, far to the south at Port Jackson (now called Sydney). Despite their fear of what might await them, Bligh's crew were euphoric at the prospect of reaching dry land. Later that day, they made landfall at a deserted, offshore island that Bligh christened Restoration Island. Many of the men were so weak they could hardly stand, but others tore at oysters on the rocks, guzzling down as much as they could eat.

Later that day, in a copper pot taken from the *Bounty*, they cooked a delicious stew with oysters and pork. Each man had a whole 500ml (one pint) to himself. As they ate, Bligh cautioned his men not to eat the fruits and berries that surrounded them. All were unknown to Europeans, and some were bound to be poisonous. But many of the men chose to ignore his warning. On board the boat Bligh's expert seamanship and gallant attempts to keep the crew in good spirits commanded a grudging respect, but on land old resentments boiled up, and the good relationship he had built up with his crew evaporated.

Bitter quarrels broke out as Bligh tried to keep discipline among his men. He felt it was his duty to return everyone safely to England, and the only way to do this was to share everything they had between them. The sicker members of the party, especially, needed to be looked after. But other men, starved and exhausted after so long at sea, felt that everyone should look after themselves. They wanted to eat what they found, rather than contributing to a common share.

Bligh sensed his command was rapidly slipping from him, and took desperate measures, drawing his cutlass on one seaman who had spoken to him rebelliously. "I determined (decided) either to preserve my command or die in the attempt." he wrote in his log.

Order was restored, but it was a miserable, quarrelsome party that set sail again, on the second leg of their journey to Timor. Despite the stopover, their health and morale soon plummeted. By the time land was sighted again, after another 10 days at sea, most of the men were too weak even to cheer.

❖

So, on June 14, 1789, 47 days after the mutiny, the Union Jack was unfurled and Bligh's launch sailed into the port of Kupang. Bligh's log entry for that day is full of justifiable pride in his achievement, but he also wrote:

"Our bodies were nothing but skin and bones, our limbs were full of sores, and we were clothed in rags. In this condition, the people of Timor beheld us with a mixture of horror, surprise and pity."

From Kupang they were taken to Java, and then homeward on a Dutch merchant ship. The journey to England took nine months. Several of Bligh's men, weakened by their ordeal, died on the way. The arguing continued too. Bligh had two of his crew imprisoned aboard the ship for daring to suggest he had falsified expenses forms.

Yet, despite his obvious faults, the irascible Captain William Bligh had taken his men on an extraordinary 6,300km (3,900 miles) journey to safety, and so ensured that 11 of them would live to see their families again.

After the ordeal

Bligh returned to England to discover he was the father of twin girls, and to write a best-selling account of the *Bounty* mutiny. In the summer of 1790, he faced a court-martial for the loss of his ship, but was acquitted.

The following year he was given a new ship, *HMS Providence*, in which he returned to Tahiti and successfully transported breadfruit plants to the West Indies, where they still grow today. From this period onwards, his nickname among fellow officers was "Breadfruit" Bligh.

In 1808 he was appointed governor of New South Wales in Australia. His attempt to restrict the import of alcohol to the territory led to an army mutiny against him, and he was imprisoned by his own troops for 26 months. This did not harm his navy career, and by the time he retired he had reached the rank of rear admiral. He died, aged 63, in 1817.

Fletcher Christian, who led the *Bounty* mutiny, fled with nine other mutineers and 18 Tahitians to remote and uninhabited Pitcairn Island, in the South Pacific. Here, Christian and most of his companions met violent deaths, squabbling among themselves or with the Tahitians. Today Pitcairn Island is inhabited by 18 families. Between them they have only four surnames, three of which – Christian, Young and Brown – belong to the original mutineers.

Other members of the mutineers, who decided to stay in Tahiti, were eventually arrested when Royal Navy ships visited the island. Several of them were hung from the yard-arm of a ship – the traditional navy punishment for mutiny.

The story of the mutiny on the *Bounty* continues to fascinate, and books on the subject have been in print for the last two hundred years. At least three films have been made of the episode, most recently in 1984 as *The Bounty*, starring Anthony Hopkins as Captain Bligh and Mel Gibson as Fletcher Christian.

Bligh and Christian's different approaches to leadership and their men is now a common case study in management training courses, and the events of the mutiny are available as a computer game.

Adrift in the desert

A small plane cut a lonely path through the pitch black sky. The drone of its single propeller engine was the only sound for miles around. Below, in the impenetrable darkness, lay the vast Sahara Desert. Inside the tiny cockpit were French pilot Antoine de Saint-Exupéry and his co-pilot André Prévot. It was the day before New Year's Eve, 1935.

The two men had been flying in the dark since leaving Benghazi, Libya, four hours before. They were attempting to fly from Paris to Saigon faster than anyone before them. If they broke the record before the end of the year, they would win a prize of 150,000 francs.

Their immediate destination was Cairo, Egypt, but they should have arrived there by now. Blinking back exhaustion Saint-Exupéry, known to all as Saint-Ex, offered Prévot another cigarette. Both men strained their eyes trying to find some landmark to tell them where they might be. But beyond the wing-lights there was nothing to be seen. Surely, below, there was a river or a city that would give them a clue to their whereabouts?

They flew on, but as every minute passed, it became more and more obvious that they were completely, hopelessly lost. The fuel indicator on the aircraft instrument panel was now worryingly low, and a night-time landing in the desert would almost certainly be fatal.

❖

Then, all at once, both men spotted a lighthouse blinking in the darkness.

"Thank Heavens! We must be near to the coast. Let's go down to have a closer look," said Saint-Ex.

"Once we get a view of the coastline, I'll soon find us on the map," said Prévot, "and if I can't, then we'll just have to land next to the lighthouse and ask for directions."

The engine strained as Saint-Ex dived, but an instant later the plane smashed quite unexpectedly into the ground, shuddering violently as it plunged across the desert. Inside the cockpit the two men braced themselves for a violent, fiery death. But no explosion came, and the plane rapidly screeched to a grinding halt.

"What the devil happened there?" yelled Prévot, angrily.

"Never mind that," said Saint-Ex, "Let's get out of here before this thing blows up."

The two men scrambled out into the cool night

air and ran for their lives. When they had put a safe distance between them and the plane, they stopped to catch their breath.

"Any broken bones?" asked Saint-Ex. "No? Me neither. You're shaking like a leaf. . ."

"Just bruises by the feel of it," said Prévot. "Anyway, as I said, what the devil happened there?"

Saint-Ex looked embarrassed.

"We must have been a lot closer to the ground than I thought. But here we are. Frankly, I can't believe we're still alive, and the plane didn't go up in a fireball. Maybe there's just no fuel left in the tank?"

Prévot smiled. He too was beginning to realize how lucky they were to have survived.

"You're right, let's be grateful for that! Look at all these black pebbles on the ground. They're just like ball bearings. We must have rolled along on them. Now, where's that lighthouse?"

❖

But all around, as far as their eyes could see in the darkness, there was only desert. They listened for the comforting crash of waves lapping on a beach, but there was nothing to hear but the sound of their own breathing.

Prévot spoke first.

"That lighthouse we both saw wasn't really there,

was it?"

"Doesn't look like it," said Saint-Ex, who was beginning to feel quite worried. "Probably a reflection from the instrument panel on the cockpit window. We're in serious trouble aren't we?"

The two men wandered back to the plane to check their supplies. Their water container had burst when they crashed, its contents instantly soaked up by the arid ground. Between them they had a small flask of coffee, half a bottle of wine, a slice of cake, a handful of grapes and an orange.

As the excitement of the crash wore off, they both began to feel cold.

"Pretty chilly for a desert," said Prévot.

"Pretty bad place for a crash, my friend," said Saint-Ex. "Boiling hot by day. Freezing cold by night, and not a soul for miles around. We'll be better off inside the plane for the moment."

They crawled into the wreckage and waited for dawn. Neither man could sleep, for each was too well aware of their desperate situation. If they had crashed on a recognized flight path, they might be rescued within a week. But they were completely lost – specks in a huge, sprawling desert. A search party could spend six months looking, and still not find them. In the heat of the day, their supplies might last five hours.

"Here's a comforting thought," said Saint-Ex wryly. "I've been told that out in the desert a man can live less than a day without water. I'm beginning to wonder if we'd have been better off dying in the plane when it hit the ground."

❖

A slow dawn broke over the desert. As the darkness receded, Saint-Ex and Prévot were able to see exactly what sort of landscape they had landed in. All around, rising and falling in dunes and hillocks, black pebbles stretched to the horizon. Not a single blade of grass grew from the ground. Their surroundings looked as lifeless as the moon.

The two men studied their map forlornly. Even if they knew where they had landed, it would have offered little comfort. The vast emptiness of the desert was punctuated by the occasional symbol for a well or religious institution, but these map markings were few, and far apart.

"It looks pretty hopeless," said Prévot, "but maybe there's an oasis nearby?"

Saint-Ex nodded encouragingly. "Let's head off east before it gets too hot – we were supposed to be going that way anyway – and see what we can find."

The two wrote their plan for the day in huge 10m (30ft) letters in the ground, in case anyone should find their plane when they were gone. Then they headed off, scraping their boots behind them to leave a trail away from the plane.

They soon forgot to mark their route, and after five hours of aimless wandering, they began to worry that they would not be able to find their way back. The day wore on and the sun rose higher in the sky. The fierce desert heat grew more intense and drained the strength from their bones.

In the shimmering light, mirages too began to torment them. A faint shape on the horizon could be a fort or a town. A dark shadow to the west could be vegetation. Lakes glistened in the distance, but all vanished when Saint-Ex and Prévot approached.

After six hours, both men were terribly thirsty, and had begun to despair. Then Prévot shouted with glee, "Look! Tracks!"

"They're ours," said Saint-Ex glumly, "I just know they are. Let's follow them anyway, they'll lead us back to the plane."

Sure enough, after another hour stumbling along the path the tracks made, they returned to the wreckage of their aircraft. Here they had left the last of their supplies, and they both drank down the coffee and wine with no thought for the next day.

"Let's make a fire," said Saint-Ex. "It'll keep us warm at night, and someone may even spot it."

They dragged a piece of wing away from the plane, and doused it with left-over fuel. It burned with a thick, black smoke, which stood out starkly against the cloudless sky. Staring into the flames, Saint-Ex imagined he could see his wife's face looking up at him sadly from under the rim of her hat. Prévot too thought of his family and the grief his death would cause them.

"I do have some good news," said Saint-Ex, breaking the silence between them. "I've found some animal burrows nearby. Something is managing to live in this wilderness, so perhaps we can too. Let's set some traps before we go to bed, and maybe we'll have something to eat for breakfast."

❖

Next morning they emerged from the plane feeling full of hope. Both men had slept better and now they were determined to beat the desert. They began by wiping dew off the wings of the plane with a rag. But when they wrung out the rag, it yielded only a spoonful of liquid – a sickening mixture of water, paint and oil.

Prévot had a plan.
"They'll definitely have noticed we're missing by now, so I'm going to stay with the plane today. It's too hot to go walking about, and I want to be here to

light a fire in case a search plane goes by."

"Good idea," said Saint-Ex. "You do that and I'll go out foraging."

So that was what they did.

Saint-Ex's traps were empty, but he did notice tracks nearby. Saint-Ex thought the three-toed imprint was probably a desert fox's footprint. He followed the tracks until he came to the animal's feeding ground – a few miserable shrubs, with tiny golden snails among the branches. Saint-Ex was not desperate enough to try the snails – anyway they were probably poisonous, and there was no water to be had from the shrubs, so he pressed on.

As he trudged through the desert, thirst began to torment him terribly. The mirages began as well, although in his weakening state Saint-Ex wondered if these were actually hallucinations instead. First there was a man standing on a nearby ridge. That turned out to be a rock. Then he saw a sleeping Bedouin – a desert tribesman. Saint-Ex rushed over to wake him, but that turned out to be a tree trunk. It was so ancient it had turned into smooth black charcoal.

Then Saint-Ex saw a desert convoy of Bedouins and their camels moving along the horizon, and called out to an empty desert. A monastery, a city, the sound of the sea, all followed in succession. But

Saint-Ex was a philosophical character. Rather than be tormented by these illusions, he allowed himself to be amused. In his dazed state, he staggered around laughing at his circumstances.

The mirages faded with the dwindling light. As night fell despair swept over him again, and Saint-Ex cried out in anguish. But his voice was no more than a hoarse whisper. He returned empty-handed to Prévot, who had lit a fire to guide him back.

In the flickering light, Saint-Ex saw something that made his heart leap. Prévot was talking to two Bedouins – they had been saved! These men would give them food and water, and guide them out of the wasteland. But as Saint-Ex approached, the two strangers vanished. There was only Prévot after all.

That night they tore a parachute into six sections and laid it on the ground, covered with stones to stop the wind from blowing it away. This, they hoped, would catch the morning dew and provide them with much-needed water. They shared their final orange and sank into an exhausted sleep.

❖

At dawn the next morning, Saint-Ex and Prévot wrung out nearly two litres (four pints) of water from the parachute fabric into the only container they had – an empty fuel tank. Unfortunately their pitiful supply of life-saving water was horribly contaminated, both by the lining of the tank and by the chemicals used to treat the parachute. It was a queasy yellow-green and tasted utterly revolting. After trying to force down a couple of mouthfuls, both men spent the next fifteen minutes retching into the sand.

After the spasms subsided they sat together feeling terribly ill.

"There's no chance of a search party finding us here, is there?" said Saint-Ex. "Let's head into the unknown. I know we're probably walking to our deaths, but at least there's a chance we'll find something or someone to save us. If we stay here, we're just submissively accepting our fate. And while I'm strong enough to walk I don't want to do that."

Prévot shrugged. "You're right. What can I say? Let's go."

They headed east, for no particular reason, trudging slowly through the sand, saying nothing to save their parched throats. Baked by the scorching sun, his head held down to avoid the tormenting mirages, Saint-Ex felt as if he were pursued by a wild beast, and even imagined he could feel its breath on his face.

The day dragged by in a mildly delirious way, and by dusk they were so thirsty they could not swallow, and a thin crust of sand covered their lips. But, as the sun set, Prévot saw a lake glistening on the horizon. Saint-Ex knew this was an hallucination, but his friend was so sure what he could see was real he went staggering off to investigate.

How a mirage works

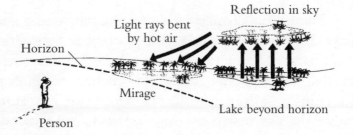

Mirages happen when light rays from objects beyond the horizon are reflected in the sky and bent by layers of warm air. This makes things look closer than they are.

Saint-Ex did not have the strength to stop him, and lay down in the sand and stones and began to daydream about the sea. He fell into a strange dream-like state and stared half-awake at the moon, which seemed to loom unnaturally large above him. Then he saw lights bobbing in the darkness – a search party come to rescue them. A figure loomed out of the dark. It was Prévot. The lights had been another hallucination. The two men began to bicker at each other's stupidity, their patience with each other and their terrible situation finally boiling over. Then they stopped.

"I guess we're in a bad way," said Prévot, his voice a hoarse rasp.

"I'm desperate for a drink," Saint-Ex whispered through cracked lips. "There must be something we can slake our thirst on."

The two had taken a medicine box with them, and now they eyed the small bottles of liquid inside it. There was alcohol, ether and iodine – all extremely poisonous ointments. Saint-Ex tried the ether, but it stung his mouth sharply. The alcohol made his throat tighten alarmingly, and one whiff of the brown iodine was enough to convince him he could not drink it.

Darkness fell, and the two men faced their first night away from the shelter of the plane. Deserts are very hot during the day, but at night they can become extremely cold, and a fierce wind swept over the two men.

"Would you believe it. I'm freezing to death!" said Saint-Ex, his teeth chattering with the cold.

Lacking any other shelter, he dug himself a shallow trough and covered his body with sand and pebbles, until only his head stuck out. As long as he stayed still, the cold did not cut into him.

Prévot tried to keep warm by walking around and stamping his feet. For him, a hole in the ground reminded him too much of a grave. He also built a feeble fire with a few twigs, but this soon went out in the fierce wind.

❖

That night seemed to last forever, and when dawn finally came it brought no dew. But at least they could still speak.

"We're OK," Saint-Ex reasoned. "When people are dying from thirst and exhaustion, their throats close up and a bright light fills their eyes. Neither of us is in that state. Let's hurry off, and travel as far as we can before the sun gets too hot."

Prévot nodded weakly. By now both men were so dehydrated they had ceased to sweat. As the sun rose in the sky, they became weaker and started to see flashes of light before their eyes. A French folksong *Aux marches du palais* (*To the steps of the palace*) played constantly in Saint-Ex's head, but he could not remember the words.

They struggled on but their legs began to buckle beneath them. The black pebbles that surrounded their plane had now given way to soft sand, which was even more difficult and exhausting to walk through. The horrible taste in their parched mouths was a constant torment. The urge to lie down in the warm sand and sink into an endless sleep was overwhelming.

But, as they stopped to rest, a sixth sense told Saint-Ex that life was nearby. A ripple of hope passed between him and Prévot, "like a faint breeze on the surface of a lake", as he recalled. Ahead were footprints. Then they heard noises. Saint-Ex saw three dogs chasing each other. But Prévot did not see them. He shook his head sadly. It was another illusion.

But it wasn't. Both men saw a Bedouin on a camel. They began shouting and waving as loudly and as wildly as their exhausted bodies would let them. But the Bedouins did not see or hear them and disappeared behind a sand dune. Then another Bedouin appeared and approached them. To the delirious men he looked like a god as he walked toward them.

Fortunately for Saint-Ex and Prévot, the Bedouin knew exactly what to do with two parched, exhausted men. Placing his hands on their shoulders he made them lie in the sand. Then he unstuck their parched lips with a feather and gently rubbed mashed lentils into their gums, to moisten their mouths. Only then did the Bedouin allow them to drink from a basin of water, but he had to keep pulling back their heads, as if they were two over-eager dogs, to stop them from drinking too fast. Later, Saint-Ex would reflect that he and Prévot were lucky not to have stumbled on some source of water on their own. In their delirious state they would have drunk frenziedly, and split their parched mouths open.

The two exhausted airmen were placed on a camel and taken to a nearby settlement. From here they were able to make their way back to France. Their final desperate gamble had paid off. Against all expectations, they had survived for over three days in the fierce heat of the desert.

After the ordeal

Following his desert rescue, Saint-Ex spent the rest of his life continuing to enhance his reputation as both a writer and pioneer aviator. His experiences in the Sahara are recounted in his book *Terre des hommes* (*Wind, Sand and Stars*) published in 1939, on which this survival story is based. His most famous book, *Le Petit Prince* (*The Little Prince*) was published in 1943. It tells the story of a pilot who crashes in the Sahara, and who meets a magical prince.

During World War Two, Saint-Ex served in the French Air Force, and fled to New York when France was defeated. Returning to serve in the Free French Forces in North Africa, he was shot down and killed during a reconnaissance flight over Corsica. He was 44. After his death, the French government awarded him the medal of *Commandeur de la Légion d'Honneur.*

Shark's breakfast

One summer morning in 1991, a 32-year-old surfer named Eric Larsen sat astride his surfboard just off the coast of Davenport Landing, in Northern California. Alone in the water, he was enjoying a moment of solitary tranquillity, and waiting for the next big wave to ride to shore. A cool breeze blew across the surface toward the beach, and he felt glad he was wearing a rubber wetsuit and gloves to keep him warm.

But as his thoughts ebbed and flowed, he noticed a huge shape drift effortlessly beneath his board. Larsen immediately snapped out of the pleasant haze he had allowed himself to drift into, and instinctively knew he was in serious trouble. But before he could begin to swim to the safety of the shore, he felt a sharp, agonizing pain. His left leg had been seized by a Great White shark.

Capable of growing to a terrifying 5.34m (17.5ft) long and weighing an unstoppable 2,043kg (4,500lb), Great Whites are one of the most feared creatures on Earth, and in their watery world they are unrivalled. So perfect are these ocean killers they have ruled their domain since the days of the dinosaur.

Ordinarily, a Great White hunts fish, dolphins and seals, and will even chew a lump from a much larger whale. Maybe the one that was now gnawing Larsen's leg mistook him for a seal, because Great Whites usually leave humans alone.

Why he was being attacked was the last thing on Eric Larsen's mind. Without thinking, he thrust his hands down to wrench away the shark's massive jaw. The Great White's jaws slowly eased apart and Larsen was able to free his damaged leg. But, in an instant, the shark took another lunge at him, and snapped both his arms into its jagged mouth.

The Great White's triangular, serrated-edge teeth, are the biggest of all fish, and no other animal on Earth has a more powerful bite. Right now Larsen was getting a horrific close-up of this mighty mouth in action. He could see the ugly gums of the shark, whose upper jaw protruded from its uplifted snout as it bit into him. The eye sockets were eerily sightless. When it attacks, the Great White protects its eyes with a thin membrane, which closes over the eye like an eyelid at the moment it strikes.

Larsen was an exceptional athlete, and he would now need to summon every ounce of his great physical strength to save his life. First, he managed to pull his shredded right arm out of the shark's mouth, and then smashed his fist into the animal's belly. The startled shark released its grip and launched itself at Larsen's surfboard. The unfortunate surfer was tethered to his board by a short cord, and for a few frantic seconds he was dragged through the water.

❖

Then, as quickly as the shark had arrived, it was gone. Calm once again settled on the bay, and Larsen was faced with the task of returning to the shore with extremely serious injuries. His left leg and both arms were shredded to the bone, and he was bleeding badly from the main artery on his left arm. For many people, such injuries received out at sea would be a virtual death sentence, and Eric Larsen had mere minutes left to live. But Larsen had one great advantage – he was a trained paramedic, and he knew exactly what he needed to do.

First of all, he had to stay calm, although the temptation to panic and get out of the water before the shark returned was overwhelming. But instead, he swam slowly to his surfboard and struggled up onto it. Then he began to paddle slowly towards the beach. Larsen knew if he swam as quickly as possible, his heart would beat faster, and he would lose even more blood.

He also knew that the more he bled, the more likelihood there was that the shark would return. In fact, a large amount of blood in the water might even lure other cruising sharks to his board, and the luckless surfer would be devoured in a horrific feeding frenzy. Fortunately, his measured pace paid off, and he eventually reached the safety of the beach.

❖

Being on dry land was a start, but now Larsen had to find some other people to help him, and quickly. Leaving a sickly red trail of blood in the sand, he began to drag himself painfully up the beach towards a row of nearby houses, calling out for help as he made his way.

Clamping his right hand firmly over the spurting gash of his bleeding artery, Larsen also held both arms above his head, because he knew that wounds bleed less when blood has to flow against gravity. But the effort of reaching the beach and dragging himself up it had exhausted him.

Larsen had also lost so much blood that he was beginning to lose consciousness. Just as he reached the edge of the row of beach houses, his head began to spin and he collapsed. But fortunately two local residents who had heard his cries had come running out toward him.

Larsen saw his last chance for survival and summoned his final reserves of strength. He explained exactly what his two helpers needed to do. His shredded leg needed to be raised above his body, to slow down the flow of blood. He also showed one of the helpers where to press down on his arm to restrict the flow of blood still pouring from his artery.

One of the locals rushed off to call for an ambulance, which arrived within minutes. He was in a hospital accident and emergency department within an hour. Here, he was given a blood transfusion and five hours of surgery to repair the shredded muscle and bone of his arms and leg. Then he was patched up with 200 stitches. Eric Larsen, shark's breakfast, had survived to tell the tale.

After the ordeal

Despite his brush with death, Eric Larsen returned to surfing as soon as he recovered from his injuries. He credited his escape from one of nature's most ferocious predators to the unpleasant taste of his rubber wetsuit.

Although shark attacks are rare (less than 260 people in the world have been attacked by Great Whites since records began), the local surfer's website for Davenport Landing reports that shark sightings are common there. One sailboarder named Mike Sullivan fell from his board in 1995, and watched it being ripped to pieces by a shark. Fortunately he was not attacked himself.

Lucky 13

On April 11, 1970, *Apollo 13* blasted off from Earth on the 13th minute of the 13th hour of the day. More superstitious men would not have volunteered for the flight, which was the third manned mission to the Moon. But if commander Jim Lovell and his fellow astronauts Fred Haise and Jack Swigert had any lingering doubts about tempting fate with unlucky thirteen, these would have probably vanished by the evening of the second day of the trip. Things were going so smoothly that mission headquarters on Earth radioed up: "The spacecraft is in real good shape as far as we are concerned. We're bored to tears down here."

But on the morning of the third day, completely out of the blue, there was a violent explosion. In the ship's tiny command module the crew heard a loud bang and felt their craft shudder. An alarm instantly filled the capsule and control panel lights began to flash, indicating that vital power and oxygen supplies were quickly ebbing away.

The astronauts had been trained to keep a cool head, but their first radio message to NASA*

*America's space agency, the National Aeronautics and Space Administration.

80

headquarters in Houston, sounded distinctly edgy.

"OK, Houston, we've had a problem."

They'd had an extremely serious problem. An oxygen fuel tank in the service module had blown up when a heating switch malfunctioned. The trouble this caused immediately doubled when another oxygen tank linked to it also emptied out into space.

It was April 13, after all.

❖

Apollo 13's crew, and the staff at Mission Control, Houston, were baffled. At Houston, where every aspect of the flight was being closely monitored by hundreds of technicians, instrument readings suggested that either the explosion should never have happened, or it should have destroyed *Apollo 13*.

There was no emergency procedure for an accident like this. When NASA had designed the Apollo craft, many safety features and back-ups had been built in. But engineers had assumed that anything which knocked out two oxygen tanks would also destroy the spaceship. One senior engineer summed up their thinking should this happen: "You can kiss those guys goodbye." But now it had happened, and the astronauts were still very much alive.

Apollo 13

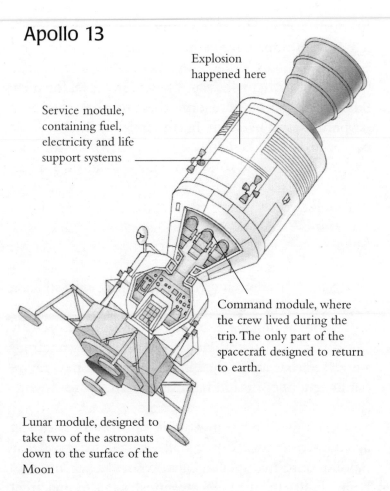

Explosion happened here

Service module, containing fuel, electricity and life support systems

Command module, where the crew lived during the trip. The only part of the spacecraft designed to return to earth.

Lunar module, designed to take two of the astronauts down to the surface of the Moon

At first Lovell, Swigert and Haise did not understand just how seriously their ship had been damaged. But 14 minutes after the explosion, Lovell noticed a cloud of white gas drifting past a command module window. This was the oxygen leaking away from the ruptured tanks. So much had been lost that it now enveloped the ship like a ghostly mist. This was the moment when Lovell realized how serious their situation actually was. They were alive, for now, but *Apollo 13* could become their tomb, locked in a perpetual orbit between Earth and the Moon.

❖

But not everything was stacked against them. Lovell, who was 42, was on his second trip to the Moon, and was America's most experienced astronaut. He had a reputation for good fortune.

"If Jim fell into a creek," said a colleague, "he'd come up with a trout in his pocket."

Even now, he was living up to his reputation. Lovell's crewmates were both new to space, but he could not have hoped for a more appropriate crew to cope with the disaster that had overtaken them. Swigert, the command module pilot, was an expert in Apollo emergency procedures. Haise, the lunar module pilot, had spent 14 months in the factory that built his spacecraft. He knew this complex machine inside out.

As *Apollo 13* continued on its Moon-bound trajectory (flight path), instruments indicating power and oxygen supplies were now all heading stubbornly to zero. The command module, which was to have been their home for the journey between Earth and the Moon and back, was close to breaking down. Lovell estimated it would only keep his crew alive for another two hours.

To survive they needed to move to the lunar module, the part of the spacecraft designed to take two men down to the Moon's surface. This part of *Apollo 13* had so far remained unused on this flight. Now hundreds of switches had to be operated to bring it to life.

Aboard the dying command module, Lovell, Swigert and Haise began these painstaking procedures. Complex coordinates were logged into the lunar module's navigation computers, life support systems whirred into operation, and instrument panels flickered into life. The men worked as quickly as they dared. A mistake made here could prove fatal.

Finally, the lunar module was ready. When they had shut down the fading power supplies of the command module, the three moved through a small connecting tunnel and into its cramped interior. But there was still much work to do. All three men now realized there was no chance of landing on the Moon. Their only priority was to get home alive. Swigert insisted their first task aboard the lunar module should be to make a course correction. This would shorten their journey by a day or so, taking them around the Moon and back to Earth as quickly as possible. So, five hours after the explosion, Lovell ignited the lunar module's engines in a 30 second burst. Everything went as intended. Now their supplies would not have to last so long.

❖

With one essential task out of the way, the crew took a long hard look at their circumstances. The lunar module had been designed to keep two men alive on the Moon for two days. Now it would have to keep three men alive for the four-day return journey to Earth.

Lovell and the crew discussed each aspect of their supplies. The situation looked like this:

Their power supplies (electricity and fuel) were looking bad. This was where the explosion had done most damage.

Their food supply was also looking grim. Most of their food was freeze-dried and needed hot water to make it edible. With their power supplies so low, hot water was no longer an option.

Their water supplies were also bad. All the craft's electronic systems generated heat, and without water to cool them they would overheat and fail.

The only thing they had in good supply was air. There should be enough of that at least, until *Apollo 13* returned to Earth.

❖

The simple truth was that the most durable items on board *Apollo 13* were the crew. They would be able to keep going on little or no heat or fuel for longer than any of the ship's equipment. The next four days were going to be very uncomfortable. Unfortunately, there was barely enough power to supply their essential equipment, so heating their spacecraft became an expendable and unaffordable luxury.

As the temperature dropped, the astronauts began to suffer. They were ill-equipped for such chilly conditions. All their clothes and sleeping bags were designed for the usually warm environment of their spaceship, and were made of thin, light materials. (The two spacesuits they carried for the Moon walk were too bulky to be worn inside the craft.) The three men improvised as best they could, wearing two sets of underwear under their jumpsuits, and Moon boots on their freezing feet.

The gnawing cold chilled the moisture in their breath, and a clammy dampness settled on the spacecraft's interior. They began to feel, said Lovell, "as cold as frogs in a frozen pool." Balanced on a knife edge between survival and death, they could not even sleep for more than two or three hours at a time, as cold and anxiety kept them awake.

Although they were constantly hungry, thirst was less of a problem. This is because astronauts do not feel the need to drink when they are in space. To conserve as much water as possible, the men drank virtually no water at all for the rest of the flight, but as a result they all became dangerously dehydrated.

❖

On the night of April 14, *Apollo 13* swung around the Moon. Inside, the crew made preparations for a second course correction, which would again involve firing the powerful lunar module engine. These engines were designed to land the module on the Moon, not propel the whole spacecraft, so once again very careful calculations had to be made. As Lovell ran through the complex procedures needed to ignite the engines, he noticed Swigert and Haise busy photographing the Moon's surface from an observation window. Suddenly, he felt very angry.

"If we don't make this next move correctly," he snapped, "you won't be getting your pictures developed."

Swigert and Haise were unrepentant.

"You've been here before," they said. "We haven't."

Despite Lovell's concerns the engine ignited successfully, and *Apollo 13* was placed on a trajectory that would take her right back to Earth. But now there was more to do than just sit and wait for their spacecraft to return. Although there was definitely enough air to get them all home, another huge problem was brewing with their breathing. Every time they breathed out, the astronauts exhaled carbon dioxide. This is a poisonous gas and, in an enclosed area such as a small spacecraft, it can soon build up to fatal levels.

All spacecraft are equipped with filters to remove this deadly carbon dioxide, but those in the lunar module were only designed to cope with the poisonous gases of two men. With all three astronauts currently occupying the lunar module, the filters were failing, and levels of the deadly gas were building up.

Back on Earth, NASA technicians had anticipated this problem, and had come up with an ingenious solution. There were several carbon dioxide filters in the now empty command module. These could be removed, placed in an airtight box, and used to filter the air aboard the lunar module.

There were no airtight boxes on board *Apollo 13*, so the crew would have to improvise. They gathered together storage bags, adhesive tape, air hoses and the covers of *Apollo 13* flight manuals. As instructions were radioed up, the three men managed to fit together a working filter, and the danger of carbon dioxide poisoning was averted.

Flight to disaster

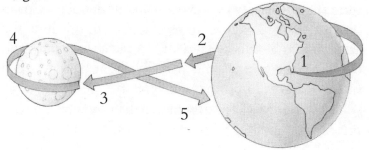

1. Lift off, April 11
2. Leave Earth's orbit, April 11
3. Oxygen tank explodes, April 13
4. Fly around Moon and return to Earth, April 14
5. Prepare for re-entry, April 17

❖

Four days after the explosion, *Apollo 13* was now well on the way home. Looking at the Earth looming ever larger in the spacecraft window, Swigert felt they were "whistling in like a high-speed train".

But the closer they got to the end of their journey, the nearer they got to its most dangerous and challenging moments. Floating in a cold spaceship, on a free-fall flight between the Moon and the Earth, was a walk in the park compared to the flight corrections they would have to make in order to land safely back on Earth.

For any spaceship, crippled or not, re-entry into Earth's atmosphere is one of the most dangerous parts of any space mission. If *Apollo 13* approached the atmosphere at too steep a flight path, then it would burn up like a meteor. But if the flight path was too shallow, it would bounce off into space, like a pebble skimming across the surface of a lake.

Not only that, but *Apollo 13* was designed to land in the Pacific Ocean. (Until the space shuttle's first flight in 1981, all American spacecraft landed at sea.) Rescue vessels had to be close at hand. To land in the right place, Lovell and his crew would have to direct their stricken craft to a minute area above the Earth's atmosphere, known as the "entry corridor". At the end of this 800,000km (500,000 mile) journey, they would have to hit a spot only 16km (10 miles) wide.

All these moves had to be made using the lunar module's engine – a task it was never designed to perform. Then the crew would have to go back into the damaged command module for the final stage of re-entry. This was the most worrying aspect of the whole procedure.

As they got closer to Earth, Lovell went back into the command module. It had been unused for four days, and was now as cold as a refrigerator. Water droplets had formed on every surface – from seat harnesses to instrument panels. Lovell wondered if the electronics behind the panels were just as waterlogged. The command module was so low on power their equipment would have to work the first time – assuming it worked at all.

❖

As Earth loomed even larger, Swigert prepared for re-entry. As pilot of the command module, it was his job to drop them into the atmosphere at the correct angle. Because they were using the lunar module engines rather than the command module to do most of the flight changes here, a whole new set of re-entry calculations and position shifts had to be prepared.

Mission Control technicians worked these out in teams and radioed the instructions up to the spacecraft. Normally, NASA would take three months to prepare such a schedule. This one they put together in two days.

In 1970 fax machines were still too primitive to be worth installing in spacecraft, and e-mails were unheard of. Swigert took two hours to write down all the hundreds of operations in full. He was not confident he would understand abbreviations in the tense moments to come. But Swigert performed brilliantly. Running though the life-or-death procedure for the first and only time, he placed *Apollo 13* exactly where it needed to be.

As re-entry drew closer, the damaged service module was finally uncoupled from the rest of *Apollo 13*. The astronauts were able to have a close look at it as it slowly drifted away from them. Here they saw for the first time the damage the explosion had done. One whole side of the module was missing, and the site of the explosion was a tangle of wires dangling from a ruptured metal cavity.

Now only the lunar module remained to be cast away. As they watched it drift off from *Apollo 13*, all three astronauts felt a strong surge of affection for the craft which had returned them safely from the Moon. Then they prepared for the most dangerous 20 minutes of their lives.

Aboard the command module, the astronauts were buffeted and rocked in their cold, damp seats, as the tiny craft began to enter the upper layers of the Earth's atmosphere. Bizarrely, it seemed to start raining inside the capsule, as the upheaval of re-entry loosened the water droplets behind the instrument panels.

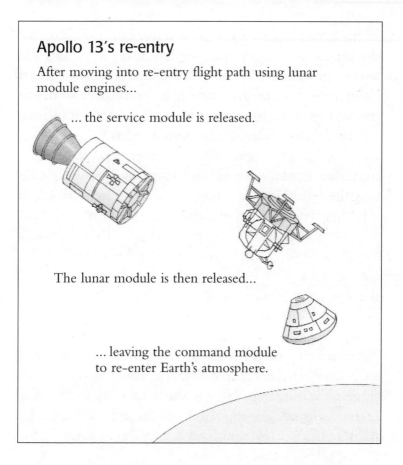

Apollo 13's re-entry

After moving into re-entry flight path using lunar module engines...

... the service module is released.

The lunar module is then released...

... leaving the command module to re-enter Earth's atmosphere.

As they plummeted down, the heat shield behind their backs began to glow red hot as it made contact with the gradually thickening air of Earth's atmosphere. Through small observation windows, the crew saw their black, star-filled view of space change to a fiery orange haze. The temperature surrounding their craft quickly reached an extraordinary 2,750°C (5,000°F).

If all went well, they should survive this stage of the journey, which would last around three minutes. But one final uncertainty lay between survival and catastrophe. After re-entry, the command module would drop through the atmosphere like a stone for a further few miles. Then, when *Apollo 13* reached 7,000m (23,00ft), parachutes would slow their craft to a safe landing speed, before they hit the sea. As they lay strapped to their seats, each man worried whether there was enough power left to operate these parachutes.

❖

Re-entry is always a time when communications between ground control and spacecraft are broken. The turbulence of the air around a blazing hot spacecraft makes it impossible to transmit radio signals. While *Apollo 13* dropped to Earth, the technicians of Mission Control waited anxiously by their consuls. Three minutes passed, then four.

Then Swigert's voice crackled over the radio, muttering a terse "OK". They had survived re-entry. Four minutes later, a rescue helicopter in the landing zone relayed live TV pictures to Houston, confirming that the parachutes on board the command module had opened. *Apollo 13* astonished the world by landing only 5.5km (3.5 miles) away from its rescue ship – the closest to date of any Apollo flight.

After the ordeal

One American newspaper remarked of *Apollo 13*'s close escape, "Never in recorded history has a journey of such peril been watched and waited out by almost the entire human race." The three astronauts arrived back at their home town of Houston, Texas, to find US president Richard Nixon waiting to greet them. None returned to space again.

James Lovell retired from NASA in 1973 to work for the Centel Corporation in Chicago. He is still regularly interviewed for TV documentaries on space flight.

Fred Haise faced another disaster in 1973, when a plane crash left him with burns over two-thirds of his body. He recovered and was at the controls of the first space shuttle when it made its maiden Earth flight in 1977, from the back of a specially modified Boeing 747 Jumbo jet. He has recently retired as President of Northrop Grumman Technical Services.

Jack Swigert took up a career in politics. He was elected to public office in Colorado in 1982, but died of bone cancer a month later.

Over the decades, the excitement and drama of the *Apollo 13* space mission was gradually forgotten, until a 1995 Hollywood film, starring Tom Hanks, brilliantly and faithfully told the story. The film was a great success, and made the surviving astronauts famous all over again.

Swallowed by a volcano

During the filming of the Hollywood thriller *Sliver* in 1992, director Phillip Noyce was searching for images to add an air of menace to his picture. He decided shots of the inside of a fiery volcano would do this effectively. After all, there are few things in nature more forbidding than a smoking volcano, all set to unleash massive destruction with a terrifying roar and rumble.

So film cameramen Michael Benson and Chris Duddy were dispatched to Hawaii's Volcanoes National Park, with instructions to capture a steaming volcano in action. Benson was a seasoned professional, and veteran of such Hollywood films as *Patriot Games* and *Terminator II*.

The volcano they chose to film was Pu'u O'o (pronounced POO-oo OH-oh). This had erupted recently and had a jagged, disfigured peak. Beneath this lurked a crater holding a steaming, bubbling cauldron of glowing lava. Corrosive, choking gases venting off the lava curled up through the massive crater, casting thick, smoky clouds which hung ominously over the volcano's summit.

Pu'u O'o was perfect. It was also so menacing that Benson and Duddy took a superstitious precaution as they embarked on their mission. Local folklore told of a fearsome goddess named Madame Pele, who was supposed to lurk within the volcano's fiery cone. Legend had it that she was very fond of gin so, as a gesture of goodwill, the two men brought a bottle with them to throw into the crater. Maybe it would ensure their safety, and good weather, while they were working?

❖

Benson and Duddy decided that Saturday November 21 would be the best day to do their filming. That morning they hired local pilot Craig Hosking, and a Bell Jet Ranger helicopter. Hosking flew them from Hawaii's Hilo Bay airfield to Pu'u O'o. The weather wasn't as good as they had hoped – it was damp and foggy, and showed little sign of clearing as they approached the ash-strewn summit. Thick, sulphurous clouds covered the volcano, making it almost impossible to see.

As the helicopter made its first pass over the volcano summit, the men looked down inside the crater. Even in the relative comfort and safety of the helicopter, they could feel the heat from the lava, and the volcano's fumes caught in their throats. When they crossed the middle of the crater, Benson lobbed in the bottle of gin. They watched it plummet down through the smoke and cloud, and imagined the green glass swallowed by the lumpy red-hot lava, and the gin vanishing in a hissing puff of steam.

Gaps in the cloud came and went, and Benson and Duddy were able to do some filming. But as the helicopter wheeled around to make a final pass over the crater before returning home, the engine started to splutter. Losing power, it began to drop into the steaming volcano.

Benson and Duddy glanced over to Hosking, who was obviously alarmed. They were now losing height rapidly, and the pilot was wrestling with his controls, desperate to avoid a landing inside the crater.

But Hosking was fighting a losing battle. Benson and Duddy sat rigid with fear as the helicopter lurched into the rim, and headed straight for a deep pool of glowing lava in the middle of the crater. Fortunately, the engine had not entirely cut out, and Hosking still had some control over his stricken craft.

As they neared the ground, the pilot directed his helicopter to a flat rock ledge above the lava pool. Coming into land they pitched and rolled, and the men were flung to and fro in their flimsy seats. Then, the still spinning rotor blades hit the ground and immediately shattered. The helicopter dropped with a sickening thud and broke in half. Benson, Duddy and Hosking, lucky not to have been hit by splintered rotor blades, staggered out from the wreckage, battered but uninjured.

Inside Pu'u O'o

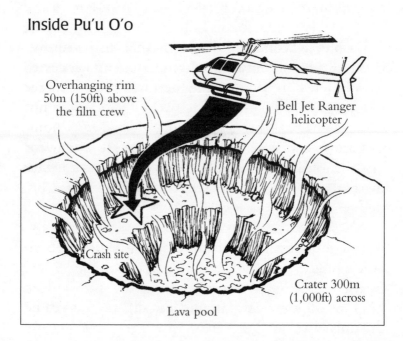

Overhanging rim 50m (150ft) above the film crew

Bell Jet Ranger helicopter

Crash site

Crater 300m (1,000ft) across

Lava pool

The ledge they had landed on was solid rock, but the heat from the molten lava below it still penetrated through their boots. Steam hissed and sputtered from cracks in the ground, threatening to scald anyone unlucky enough to be standing directly above. Clouds of dense, acrid gas drifted around them. The gas was so thick that most of the time the men could barely see their hands in front of their faces.

Then there was the terrible noise. An intense and constant roar filled the air, like the screaming engines of a jet plane, as pools of lava bubbled and boiled around them.

Each man wondered how long they could survive in this smoky inferno. Their immediate chances of rescue were not good. Inside the shattered helicopter cockpit, the radio refused to work. They were not expected back at the airfield for at least another hour, so no one would be wondering where they were for a while yet. They would have to try to make their own way out.

Above them, occasionally visible through the drifting mist, was the summit rim. It was around 50m (150ft) away.

"Let's go for the top," said Benson. "It seems to be the only way out."
But the climb was more difficult than it looked. The rocky surroundings they scrambled up regularly gave way to deep ash and crumbling stone, and the men found themselves sinking up to their knees in hot, black soot.

After 15 exhausting minutes, they had managed a whole 25m (75ft) – around halfway up the slope. Here the air was slightly clearer, and they could see the slope getting steeper, and then jutting into an overhanging rim at the top. It looked impossible to get over without proper climbing equipment.

Hosking was sure they would never make it.

"Look, I've got an idea," he told the cameramen. "We need to get help, and the only way we're going to do that is to go back to the helicopter and repair that radio."

Benson wasn't convinced.

"I think it's too dangerous. Look down – the 'copter is just covered with poisonous clouds of smoke. If you go back, you'll pass out – or worse."

But Hosking was determined.

"We've got no choice. We stay up here and choke to death. We go down there and choke to death. At least down there there's some chance I can fix the radio and call for help."

He had made up his mind. Wrapping his shirt around his face to keep off the worst of the acrid fumes, he set off back down the slope to return to the helicopter.

Benson and Duddy watched him vanish into the mist, certain they were safer where they were. But they were wrong. Hosking reached the helicopter and began to repair the radio. He could only work on it for short periods, and had to keep coming out of the wreckage to climb to a clearer spot above, to breathe in fresher air. But, piece by piece, he put the radio back together. He also took a battery from one of Duddy and Benson's cameras, and hooked it up to the radio. After a difficult hour, the radio began to crackle. Then a steady roar of static could be heard above the volcano's din, and Hosking knew he'd fixed it.

He tuned into the airfield frequency and was soon speaking to colleagues back at Hilo Bay. An hour later, helicopter pilot Don Shearer, who had often worked on rescue missions in Hawaii, was flying over the volcano.

Shearer radioed down to Hosking.

"Can't see a thing down there, Craig. Smoke's too thick. You're gonna have to guide me in."

"Good to hear you!" said a relieved Hosking, who was now beginning to believe he would get out of this disaster alive. "OK, message understood. I can hear you, so I'll guide you down."

Peering blindly through the swirling smoke, Hosking could faintly hear the dull throb of rotor blades. Gradually he was able to get Shearer to fly close enough to be able to spot the wreckage. As the craft hovered a couple of feet above the ground,

Hosking ran up to it and leaped inside. Clouds of smoke swirled away beneath him as the helicopter lifted him to safety. He, at least, had escaped the clutches of Madame Pele.

❖

Crouching on a ledge halfway up the crater, Benson and Duddy had heard the helicopter arrive, although they could not see it through the smoke. They were disappointed to hear its engines recede into the distance, but were pleased to know that at least something was being done to find them.

Hope was closer at hand than they realized. Hosking's radio signals had been picked up by the local National Park rangers. Two rangers had climbed to the tip of the rim and were trying to spot the helicopter crew. The atmosphere around the summit was so deadly they had to wear gas masks, and acidic fumes were corroding their climbing ropes. Every so often, they shouted down into the crater, to try to make contact with the stranded men.

Benson and Duddy heard these faint shouts from their would-be rescuers, above the roar of the lava pits. They sprang to their feet, waving frantically and shouting themselves hoarse. But the cloudy fumes inside the crater were too thick, and their muffled voices just echoed all around the huge rim, making it impossible for either the rescuers or the trapped men to locate each other.

The rangers gave up trying to find the men by shouting. Instead they threw down ropes, in the vague hope that one would land near Benson and Duddy. But the rim of the crater was 300m (1,000ft) across. It was like trying to find a needle in a haystack.

Eventually, darkness fell, and further searching was useless. The rangers gave up, intending to return the next morning.

❖

During the night it rained torrentially, and Benson and Duddy shivered in their soaking clothes. But the rain at least brought some relief from the scorching heat in the crater. When morning came, the weather was even worse. This made a helicopter rescue increasingly difficult. Besides, Don Shearer found that his helicopter had been damaged by the volcano's corrosive fumes when he rescued Hosking, and was now unsafe to fly. Back at the rim of the crater, the rangers could hardly see 3m (10ft) in front of them.

The day wore on, and Benson and Duddy realized they were facing the prospect of another night in the crater, alternately baked by glowing lava and frozen by lashing rain. Choked by fumes, their eyes streaming, the two had only their shirts to wrap around their faces to protect themselves from the poisonous surroundings.

By mid-afternoon of that second day inside the crater, Duddy's patience snapped.

"Maybe there's another way out?" he said to Benson. "Instead of sitting here waiting to be rescued, we ought to be trying to get out ourselves. Whatever, trying to escape is better than sitting here suffocating."

Benson was not convinced. Older and not as fit as Duddy, he doubted his ability to climb further up the slope of the crater to the overhanging rim.

"You go then, Chris," he said, "I'm going to have to stay here."

Benson watched Duddy set off up the slope, and slowly disappear into the cloudy smoke. Inside the crater the light was slowly fading, and now Benson faced a second night in the crater, this time on his own. Duddy did not return. Benson began to think his friend had succeeded, but then he saw a shape fall through the mist. Convinced it was Duddy plunging to his death, Benson was consumed with a terrible mixture of misery, exhaustion and guilt. "Why did I ever bring us to this awful spot?" he said to himself. Weak from lack of food and sleep, he wondered how much longer he could survive.

But, in fact, Duddy had struck lucky. After an exhausting climb through crumbling rock and sooty gravel, he eventually reached a section of the rim where he could scramble out. He soon met up with the rangers who were trying to find them both. They all shouted down to Benson, but their voices were lost in the huge, hollow cauldron.

With night falling, and for want of anything better to do, the rangers tossed food and water packets into the crater, hoping that Benson might stumble upon one. Benson did indeed see one of these packets from a distance. It was this he thought was Duddy plunging to his death.

Luck was not with Michael Benson that night, and he did not find any of these food and water packets. Getting weaker by the hour, breathing was now a painful effort. His mouth was also so dry he could no longer call for help, and the fumes were causing him to hallucinate. He battled with a raging thirst, catching rain in the face of his camera light-meter, and drinking it a mouthful at a time.

Another day dawned. Benson, curled up in a shivering ball, wondered if he would live to see the end of it. But away from the volcano, further action was being taken to rescue him. Overnight, Hosking and Duddy had managed to contact another helicopter pilot named Tom Hauptman, who was famed for his daring rescues. Soon after first light, Hauptman flew over the crater rim. For the first time, through a gap in the clouds, Hauptman managed to spot Benson. The ailing cameraman had heard the helicopter. He was standing up and waving frantically.

Hauptman's helicopter was equipped with a large net, which could be lowered below the craft. Benson was now obscured by cloud again, and Hauptman felt as if he was fishing in a muddy pool. The net went down once, then twice, each time coming back empty. But, on the third attempt, the net landed right in front of the ailing cameraman. Benson grabbed his chance, and threw himself into the net. The helicopter pulled up, and he was lifted away from the crater. Lying in the net, Benson felt deliriously happy. He had escaped from Madame Pele after all.

After the ordeal

Hauptman dropped Benson off with the park rangers, who bundled him into an ambulance and took him to Hawaii's Hilo Hospital. Having been exposed to the volcano's poisonous fumes for over 48 hours, he had seriously damaged his lungs. Fortunately, he was able to make a full recovery. Duddy and Hosking, by comparison, escaped with fairly minor injuries.

The rangers who rescued Benson are convinced he has set a world record for the length of time anyone has managed to survive inside an active volcano.

The film *Sliver* was completed without any shots of smoking volcanoes. One leading character in the film does confess, however, to a great fascination with volcanoes, and admits he has fantasies about flying into one.

Don Shearer and Tom Hauptman, the pilots who flew rescue helicopters into Pu'u O'o, are both thanked in the film's credits.

Terror in the sky

On a crisp December morning in 1942, a Boston bomber took off from Wayzata airfield, Minnesota, USA. Aboard were 29-year-old American test pilot Sid Gerow, and Canadian test observer Harry Griffiths, who was 20.

The aircraft had come to them straight from the factory. It was their job to give it a thorough check-over before it made the long journey across the Atlantic to England, where it would be used to fight in World War Two.

The craft climbed into a cloudless sky, and when it reached 2,100m (7,000ft) the two men began a series of checks and tests. Gerow tried out the controls, pulling the Boston into a slight dive and turning to the left and right, while Griffiths stood beside him, monitoring the instrument panel. Then they tried the two engines, running them at maximum speed, and then pulling back until the Boston was going so slowly, it nearly dropped from the sky.

"No problems here. Everything looks pretty good," shouted Griffiths over the roar of the engines.

He had gone through this drill hundreds of times, and was completely in tune with the workings of the Boston. He knew every rattle and hum of the engines, and every strut and panel of the fuselage, like the back of his hand.

Gerow made a thumbs up gesture in response.

"When you've checked the bombsight I'll take her down," he said.

Griffiths moved swiftly down from the cockpit to the forward section of the plane. The nose of the Boston bomber was made almost entirely of transparent acrylic, giving the bomb aimer an excellent view both of the ground beneath and the skies around the aircraft. Griffiths crouched down and lay flat on his stomach, peering into the telescopic viewer on the bombsight, which was set at the very tip of the bomber's nose.

But, as he checked the mechanism, Griffiths felt the floor beneath him give way. In the Boston, the bomb aimer had to lie across the forward entry hatch to work the bombsight, but the lock on the hatch was obviously faulty.

❖

As he fell through the floor Griffiths instinctively grabbed at the bombsight with both hands, but an immense gust of freezing air sucked the rest of his body out of the aircraft. With the wind and the throb of the Boston's two engines roaring loudly in his ears, he found himself hanging halfway out of the plane, his legs and lower body pressed hard against the fuselage. He yelled at the top of his voice: "Geeeerrrrooooowwwww!!!!", but knew immediately that there was almost no chance his crewmate could hear him.

Clutching at the bombsight had saved him from plummeting directly out of the aircraft, but the wind was pulling hard at his body, and his fingers soon lost their grip on the polished metal instrument. As his head slipped out of the plane, he clutched desperately at the wooden fitting beneath the sight. Outside the plane the temperature was -25°C (-13°F) and fierce cold gnawed at his battered body.

Harry Griffiths was small, but he was immensely strong. He wrapped his fingers around the wooden fitting and held on with a vice-like grip. Buffeted mercilessly by the plane's turbulent slipstream, few other men could have clung to such a precarious position.

But cling he did, for Harry Griffiths had no other choice. His strength was slowly leaving him and he called feebly for help, but his cries were snatched away by the fierce wind. Very soon his grip would weaken, and he would slip out of the plane and fall to his death.

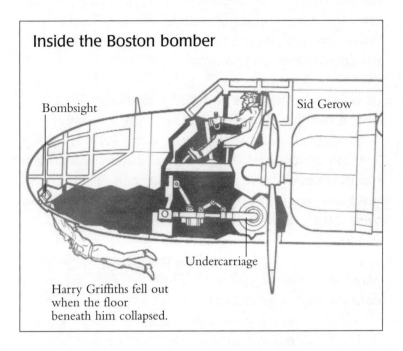

Inside the Boston bomber

Bombsight

Sid Gerow

Undercarriage

Harry Griffiths fell out when the floor beneath him collapsed.

In the cockpit above the open hatch, Sid Gerow knew exactly what had happened the moment cold air billowed into the plane, and a severe wind howled around his boots.

"Hey Griffiths, are you all right there?" he shouted down.

There was no reply to his urgent inquiries, but Gerow imagined he could hear his comrade's faint shouts for help. What could he do?

Gerow thought fast. He was in a very difficult situation. If Griffiths had not fallen clean out of the plane, and was clinging on as he suspected, there was little the pilot could do to help. He could not leave the controls of the Boston, for without him the plane would plummet to the ground.

What about an emergency landing? This too would not help Griffiths. In the Boston bomber, the front wheel of the undercarriage was directly beneath the cockpit and in front of the forward entry hatch. If Gerow lowered the wheel it would dislodge his dangling companion. Surely there was something he could do to save Griffiths's life?

As he flew on, the sun caught the frozen waters of Lake St. Louis 2,100m (7,000ft) below. The glare momentarily dazzled, but as it did so inspiration struck. Gerow pushed his control column down, sending the Boston into a dive. He headed directly toward the lake, approaching it as low and as slow as he dared. Anyone falling from a speeding plane onto earth or water would be killed for sure, but ice. . . maybe that would be different?

❖

Beneath the plane, Griffiths was fighting for his life, and struggling just to keep breathing. He was numb with cold, and his grip was going. But as he saw the lake loom before him, he knew at once what he needed to do. The Boston was now skimming over the smooth ice, which was racing below him at 160kmph (100mph). Griffiths knew Gerow could not go any slower, as the plane would stall and both men would be killed.

Griffiths hesitated, plucking up his courage for this last desperate gamble to save his life. Then he let his frozen fingers loosen from the plane. He half expected to drop like a stone, but for a brief moment he glided above the surface, hurled along by his own velocity.

Then he hit the ice with a sickening thud, which completely knocked the breath from his body. Instinctively, he curled into a ball and careered across the frozen surface, hoping that he would not hit a half-submerged log or any other kind of obstacle that would kill him in an instant. Gerow had been right about ice. Its slipperiness prevented the sudden impact that would have killed Griffiths. Gradually, his speed across the ice began to lessen, and eventually he slowed to a halt.

Circling above, Gerow reckoned his crewmate had slid a whole 1km (half a mile). He saw the tiny figure come to a stop and lie quite still. But then, miraculously, he hauled himself to his feet and began to walk cautiously toward the shore.

After the ordeal

Sid Gerow's quick thinking and Harry Griffiths's tough flying overalls had saved his life. He was rushed to the nearest hospital, where he went into a dazed stupor. The next eight days of his life were a complete blank. But, apart from severe bruising and mild frostbite, he survived his extraordinary ordeal without serious injury.

Lost in a polar wilderness

It would be difficult to imagine a more hopeless situation. In November 1915, 29 men stood on the frozen Weddell Sea in the Antarctic, 1,900km (1,200 miles) away from the nearest human settlement. Before them lay the mangled remains of their ship *Endurance*. Especially built to withstand the harsh seas and drifting pack ice of the Antarctic, *Endurance* had been built of greenheart – a wood heavier than iron. But the ship had become caught in the ice a mere day's sailing away from the Antarctic coast. Now, after months of relentless pressure, the hull was being crushed by the ice.

As the crew stood a safe distance away, *Endurance* screeched and groaned in such an eerie fashion, many of the men watching thought she sounded like a dying animal. As the hull gave way, the boat collapsed. Over the last few days, all of the useful equipment and supplies on board had been taken off and placed on the ice. Now all that remained of their boat was a tangled mess of wood, wire, rigging and metal, slowly sinking into the icy water.

Marooned in one of the worst environments on Earth, with no radio and no chance at all of human help, many people would have given up in despair. But the crew of the *Endurance* had one priceless asset – the man who had led them there in the first place. His name was Sir Ernest Shackleton, but everyone just called him "the Boss".

❖

Shackleton was a professional adventurer. He had been to the Antarctic before with the ill-fated British explorer Robert Falcon Scott, who died there in 1912. When Shackleton was not exploring, he made a living writing books and giving lectures about his expeditions. In the late 19th and early 20th centuries, explorers such as Shackleton excited great public interest, making highly dangerous expeditions to the world's wildest places. By 1914, though, there were few challenges left. Although the South Pole had been reached in 1912, no one had ever crossed the Antarctic. Shackleton, now aged 40, was determined to make this 2,415km (1,500 mile) journey, and announced plans to lead the grandly named "Imperial Trans-Antarctic Expedition" to do this.

Five thousand letters of application immediately flooded into Shackleton's central London headquarters in Burlington Street. He had already decided on some of the key members of his expedition, picking men who had worked with him before. But the rest of his crew he picked on instinct, often taking just seconds to hire complete strangers.

Expedition scientist Reginald James, for example, was asked if his teeth were good, if he had a good temper, and if he could sing. When James looked bewildered by this question, Shackleton explained that he wanted someone who could "shout a bit with the boys". On a trip like this, getting along with other people was just as important as scientific expertise.

Endurance's captain Frank Worsley joined the team after a strange dream. "One night I dreamed that Burlington Street was full of ice blocks and that I was navigating a ship along it," he later wrote. Next morning he went at once to Burlington Street where a sign saying "Imperial Trans-Antarctic Expedition" caught his eye. Worsley remembered: "Shackleton was there, and the moment I set eyes on him I knew he was a man with whom I would be proud to work." "The Boss" hired him on the spot, and Worsley became one of the expedition's most valuable members.

❖

The hand-picked crew of seamen, scientists and craftsmen left London in the late summer of 1914, just as the First World War was beginning. Also aboard were 70 dogs to pull their sleighs, and a cat called Mrs. Chippy. On the trip down to the Antarctic they were joined by a stowaway – an 18-year-old Canadian named Percy Blackboro. When Blackboro was discovered, he was brought before Shackleton, who told him, "If anyone has to be eaten, you'll be the first."

When the *Endurance* reached Antarctic waters, icebergs soon surrounded the ship. As they sailed gingerly through, Shackleton described their surroundings as "a gigantic and interminable jigsaw". But shortly after crossing the Antarctic circle, the ice closed in and packed itself tightly around them. They were stuck "like an almond in a piece of toffee", remembered one crew member. Soon they could move neither forward nor backward, and there they stayed for nine months, waiting for the ice to clear.

Although conditions on board the *Endurance* were cramped but comfortable, this was a terrible place to be stranded. Not only was it immensely cold, but at that time of year in the Antarctic, there were only a few minutes of light a day.

In previous voyages, sailors whose ships became trapped in pack ice had fallen prey to deep depression or madness, brought on by this relentless darkness. On one stranded ship in the 1890s, this madness turned men deaf and dumb, or made them hide, thinking the others were trying to kill them. Most spent the time walking in a wide oval on the deck, in what became known as the "madhouse promenade".

Shackleton was determined this would never happen to his crew. *Endurance*, for example, had been equipped with a well-stocked library precisely in anticipation of such a wait. "The Boss" also kept his crew busy organizing dog training, soccer and hockey matches, party games and lectures. The men even carved elaborate, beautiful dog kennels from blocks of ice.

❖

But, despite their patience, the ship never did break out of its icy prison. Now it had sunk, and the members of the crew were forced to camp out on the frozen sea. Surrounded by an untidy mixture of three lifeboats, salvaged equipment and supplies, they christened their new home "Camp Dump". Every one knew they were too far from civilization to be rescued.

A couple of days after the ship sank, Shackleton gathered his companions around him. If they were to survive, he told them, drastic measures were called for. But he had a plan which had every chance of success.

121

Their only option, he explained, was to haul their lifeboats through the ice to the open sea, and then sail 1,300km (800 miles) back to a whaling station at South Georgia, the nearest inhabited island. To have any chance of success, they would have to leave almost everything behind. Each man, in fact, could only bring 1kg (2lbs) of his own possessions, plus a sleeping bag, a metal cup, knife and spoon, and the heavy clothes he stood in.

To emphasize this point, Shackleton threw to the ground his watch and chain, and a pocketful of gold coins. Then, to everyone's amazement, he also threw down a Bible the Queen had given him at the start of the expedition. He could not have made his point more clearly.

On top of this single kilogram, men were allowed to keep their diaries. Shackleton felt it would be good for morale for each man to record their forthcoming struggle in detail. Leonard Hussey, the expedition meteorologist, was told he should keep his banjo, as a sing–song was always good for morale.

One of the most difficult decisions about what to take and what to leave faced the expedition photographer Frank Hurley. In the days before celluloid film, photographs were made on glass plate negatives, which were twice the size of this page, and very heavy. Shackleton and Hurley chose the best shots between them and smashed the rest, to remove the temptation of taking them all back.

But another, even harder decision also had to be made. Food supplies were so limited that there would not be enough both for the members of the expedition, and most of the animals they had brought along. Some of the dogs, and the ship's cat, had to be shot. It was kinder than abandoning them and leaving them to starve to death, but some of the men had become so attached to the ship's animals, they broke down in tears.

❖

By the time the expedition was ready to set off on their trek, it was almost Christmas, and well into the Antarctic summer. Shackleton, impatient to begin, decided they would celebrate Christmas on December 22, then leave the next day. Despite the shortages, a huge feast of ham, sausage, jugged (stewed) hare, pickles and peaches was prepared. It was a wonderful send-off. The men, fortified by their food, and in good spirits, loaded the boats and sleighs and began towing them toward the sea.

Hauling it all was hot, exhausting work, even in the Antarctic, so most of the travel was done at night when the temperature dropped below zero. But in the first five days they managed only 14km (nine miles). Shackleton's men became grumpy and dispirited, especially when sickness swept through the party. A few of the dogs they had spared were unable to pull the boats and sleighs through the rough, icy landscape, so they too had to be shot. Things were going very badly, right from the start. Fierce arguments broke out between the crew and "the Boss", and Shackleton even had to remind mutinous men that their pay, which they would all receive in a lump sum at the end of the expedition, could be stopped.

Somehow Shackleton managed to drive them on, and for three months the Trans-Antarctic Expedition slogged through the pack ice, stubbornly determined to emerge from the polar wilderness alive. But, slowly and surely, their food and fuel supplies dwindled until they were almost gone, and still the men had not reached the sea.

Then, one morning, their luck changed. A huge leopard seal poked its head out of a crack in the ice and stared at Seaman Thomas McLeod. Both eyed the other as a potential meal, but McLeod was sharper. He began flapping his arms like a penguin – the seal's juiciest prey. It lumbered out of the ice and began chasing him, and was quickly shot. This was a godsend for the expedition. Along with their scant supplies, they had been living off tiny Adele penguins, which were too small to provide much nourishment. Seal meat made a welcome change, and there was also now plenty of blubber – which they could burn in their stoves as fuel. The leopard seal that had chased Thomas McLeod had 50 undigested fish in its stomach, which was an unexpected bonus.

❖

Finally, in early April 1916, Shackleton's men came to the end of the ice and reached the open ocean. After months of pushing and trudging, they were finally able to board their three lifeboats and put to sea. But, although the hauling was over, life was no better. The boats were small, crammed with men and provisions, and open to the worst weather imaginable. At night, if the men slept in the boats, schools of killer whales would surround them. If they set up camp on an ice floe, the ice would sometimes crack. Sleeping men would plunge into the freezing sea, and had to scramble out before the ice closed above them.

They spent 12 days freezing and soaked to the skin, constantly bailing water from their boats, in a desperate effort to keep them from sinking. Eventually, land was sighted. But this was not South Georgia, as they had hoped, but Elephant Island, which was much further west. They were still 1,100km (700 miles) from South Georgia, and other human beings.

Despite it all, the men were deliriously happy. They had survived an appalling journey and, for the first time in nearly one and a half years, they could rest their feet on solid ground.

Elephant Island was a narrow 37km (23 miles) long crop of bare rock. There were no trees, but there were plenty of birds and elephant seals to eat. As the expedition lacked any other shelter, the two smaller boats the men had sailed to the island were turned upside down and made into huts. These huts were primitive but comfortable. The boats were placed on stones, and gaps were filled with moss and fabric to make them windproof. Stoves were placed inside to provide a little heat, and even small windows were carefully built into the sides of the huts, from glass salvaged from other equipment.

Although the *Endurance* expedition never did run out of food, everyone became terribly bored with their monotonous diet. During the day they would huddle around a blubber stove and fantasize aloud about trifles and sticky puddings. At night they dreamed of salads and scrambled eggs.

❖

No one would find them on Elephant Island, as it was too remote, so Shackleton decided to take the biggest boat, the James Caird, and a small crew, to try to reach South Georgia. The rest of his men would have to wait on the island for rescue.

One of Shackleton's greatest talents as a leader was his ability to pick the right people for a job, and for this trip he chose a mixture of the most able and most troublesome men. These he took with him to prevent them from annoying the men that would be left behind on Elephant Island.

Patched up with canvas and paint from the supplies of expedition painter George Marsten, the James Caird and a crew of six set out to travel 1,100km (700 miles) to the whaling station at Grytviken in South Georgia. Once again they had to battle through blizzards and gales. And again they were constantly soaked and freezing, but this time they all suffered from raging thirst, as salt water had contaminated their water supply.

After 17 days at sea, the James Caird finally reached South Georgia. But, just off the coast, a terrible gale ripped away their rudder. Unable to steer the boat, they were washed up on the side of the island furthest away from the whaling station.

❖

South Georgia was long and narrow, like Elephant Island, but it was also very mountainous. As the boat was no longer fit to sail, and the walk around the coast was over 240km (150 miles), Shackleton decided they would have to go over these uncharted mountains.

So, on May 19, 1916, taking only 15m (50ft) of rope and a carpenter's blade, Shackleton, *Endurance*'s captain Frank Worsley, and officer Thomas Crean began their climb into the unknown. Two other men, who were too weak to go on, were left behind with a third to look after them.

Shackleton, Worsley and Crean pressed on through the mountains, up and down for two days, one time tobogganing down a steep ice slope on their coiled-up rope, another time climbing down a waterfall. Once, when they stopped to rest, Shackleton let them sleep for five minutes, and then woke them, telling them half an hour had passed.

On May 21, at 7:00 in the morning, the men heard a factory whistle at Grytviken whaling station. For the first time since December 1914, here was evidence that other human beings were close by. This was the moment they realized they had escaped from the Antarctic with their lives. Their spirits lifted and they arrived at Grytviken by 1:00 that afternoon.

As they walked toward the factory, two small boys, terrified by the sight of these ragged men, ran away screaming. Shackleton asked to be taken to the home of factory manager Thoralf Sorlle, whom he knew well. Sorlle gawped at them in astonishment and said, "Who on Earth are you?" Like everyone at Grytviken, he had assumed that the *Endurance* had been lost with all aboard nearly two years before. When Shackleton told him their tale, Sorlle burst into tears.

Despite the extreme hardship of their voyage to South Georgia, and their dangerous trek through the mountains, a hot bath and a hearty meal was all Shackleton's party needed before they set off to rescue their stranded companions on the other side of South Georgia. These men were picked up the next day, but the rest of the expedition, stranded on Elephant Island, would be more difficult to reach.

Shackleton sailed out on a relief ship on May 23, but ice blocked his route. He made a second attempt to reach the island shortly afterward, but was driven back by fog. On the third attempt rough weather forced them to turn back.

Finally, after 14 frustrating weeks, Shackleton and his relief ship reached Elephant Island on August 30, 1916. A small boat was launched toward the shore, and Shackleton, standing on its bow, anxiously counted the 22 men he had left behind. They were all there. At least no one had died.

The four month wait on Elephant Island had been a tedious ordeal – best summed up in a diary entry by one of *Endurance*'s officers, Lionel Greenstreet: So passes another miserable rotten day.

Although the men had suffered from infections and boils, the only real casualty of the entire two-year adventure had been the ship's stowaway, Percy Blackboro. He had lost the toes of his left foot to frostbite. Shackleton had managed, through good judgment, and great leadership, to bring his entire expedition back alive.

After the ordeal

Shackleton was justifiably proud of his achievement. He wrote in his account of the adventure that they had been through terrible times and yet not a single life had been lost. The survivors of Shackleton's Imperial Trans-Antarctic Expedition returned home to a Europe ensnared in the horrors of World War One. Their story, which then must have seemed like a foolhardy venture, excited little interest when millions of men were dying in the trenches.

Almost all the *Endurance* crew volunteered for the armed services and two, a junior officer and a seaman, were killed in action. Shackleton, his deputy Frank Wild, and *Endurance's* captain Frank Worsley were sent to the North Russian front, where their knowledge of polar conditions would be useful to Britain's ally Russia. Many of *Endurance*'s crew served on minesweepers.

In 1921, Shackleton returned to the Antarctic, with many of his *Endurance* shipmates, on yet another expedition. He died of a heart attack at Grytviken, South Georgia, in January, 1922, and is buried on the island.

South Georgia was not crossed again for nearly 40 years. A British expedition of experienced, well-equipped climbers finally crossed the mountains again in 1955.

Today, Shackleton and his extraordinary story still continues to fascinate. Bookshop shelves are still full of Shackleton biographies and accounts of the voyage of the *Endurance*, many of them lavishly illustrated with Frank Hurley's beautiful, haunting photographs. Exhibitions, TV documentaries, and even a recent Hollywood movie keep his story alive. His brilliant leadership skills are even studied in business training courses. Shackleton "defines what you'd like people to do in a crisis", says one New York business guru. "Don't be afraid to change your plans. Don't be afraid to do nothing when that's the best thing to do. Prepare, prepare, prepare. Plan, plan plan."

"The Mighty Hood"

In the chilly waters of the North Atlantic, just below the perpetual ice field of the Arctic Ocean, a grey May dawn broke before 2:00am. Pitching through a rolling grey sea, scything wind and flurries of snow, a great grey battleship headed relentlessly toward its prey. The year was 1941.

The ship was *HMS Hood* – the most famous vessel in the British Navy. For 20 years the *Hood* had been the world's largest battleship. She had toured the oceans as a symbol of Britain's naval power, and was known all over the world as "The Mighty Hood".

The 1,421 men on board the *Hood* had been ready for battle throughout the night. Most had found it impossible to sleep, for they were about to engage in a life or death struggle with two of Germany's most powerful warships – *Bismarck* and *Prinz Eugen* – which had been sent out to the Atlantic to hunt for British cargo ships.

High above the deck, in the dimly lit compass platform, sat Vice-Admiral Lancelot Holland. Surrounded by his chief lieutenants – the ship's captain, and navigation, signal and gunnery officers – Holland scoured the horizon, his fingers tapping anxiously on his binoculars.

Waiting on the *Hood*'s masters in this lofty perch was 18-year-old signalman Ted Briggs. His job was to carry messages to other parts of the ship. Briggs had first set eyes on the *Hood* on a trip to the Yorkshire coast in 1935, when he was 12. It was love at first sight, and he had decided then and there to join the Navy to sail on her. Now, six years later, here he was, watching the calm deliberations of her senior officers with a mixture of fear and fascination.

The *Hood* had never before had to fight another ship. Briggs knew it would be a bloody, dangerous business, but he was confident that his beloved *Hood,* and the battleship *Prince of Wales*, which was sailing alongside her, would soon destroy any ship that crossed their path.

But Briggs's faith in the *Hood* was misplaced. *Bismarck* was the most powerful ship in the German fleet. Heavily armed and well protected, the aggressive angles and sweep of the ship made a striking contrast with the stately elegance of the *Hood*. Like the *Hood*, she was over $\frac{1}{4}$km ($\frac{1}{6}$ mile) long, but she was also 20 years younger, and the very model of modern naval technology. Compared to the *Bismarck*, the *Hood* looked quaintly old-fashioned.

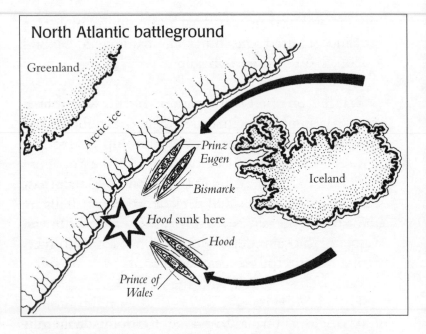

North Atlantic battleground

Greenland

Arctic ice

Prinz Eugen

Bismarck

Iceland

Hood sunk here

Hood

Prince of Wales

The two German ships were sighted at 5:35am. Ominous black dots 27km (17 miles) away, they would soon be within range of the *Hood's* huge guns. The British and German ships continued to speed toward each other, and 23 minutes later, at 5:58am, and at 20km (13 miles) apart, the battle began. *Hood* opened fire, her shells hurtling toward *Bismarck* and *Prinz Eugen* at over twice the speed of sound. Nearly half a minute passed before huge plumes of water, as high as tower blocks, rose around the two approaching ships. The *Hood* had missed.

Up on the compass platform, Briggs watched the *Bismarck's* guns return fire. Gold flashes with red cores winked from the distant ship. A low whine built to a howling crescendo, as the shells made a 20 second journey between the two ships.

Briggs's terrified anticipation ended when four huge columns of foam erupted to the right of the ship. Then an explosion knocked him off his feet.

The *Hood* had been hit at the base of her mainmast and fire spread rapidly. On deck, anti-aircraft shells set alight by the heat exploded like firecrackers. On the compass platform, the screams of wounded men trickled from the voice-pipes that kept the ship's commanders in touch with their vessel.

As the *Hood* turned to give all four of its main gun turrets a better view of the approaching enemy, another huge explosion rocked the ship, and Briggs was again thrown off his feet. A shell from *Bismarck* had penetrated deep within the hull and detonated the *Hood*'s main ammunition supplies.

Aboard the *Prince of Wales*, the men saw an eerily silent explosion – like a huge red tongue – shoot four times the height of the ship. Pieces of the mainmast, a huge crane and part of a gun turret tumbled through the air.

When Briggs got up he felt in fear for his life and knew instinctively that his ship had been fatally damaged. The *Hood* listed slowly to the right and the helmsman shouted through the voice-pipe that the ship's steering had failed.

To Briggs's relief, the *Hood* rolled slowly back to level. But this relief was short-lived. The ship lurched to the left and began to roll over. What Briggs, and no one else on the compass platform could know, was that the *Hood* had been broken in two by the explosion. The rear of the ship had sunk almost immediately, and now the rest was being claimed by the sea.

There was no order to abandon ship. As the floor became steeper and steeper, the crew on the compass platform headed unprompted to the exit ladder. An officer stood aside to let Briggs go first. Slumped in his chair, Vice-Admiral Lancelot Holland sat stunned and defeated.

❖

Briggs climbed down a ladder to a lower deck on the tilting ship, but the sea was already gushing around his legs. With desperate haste he began to shed any clothing that would weigh him down, managing to discard his steel helmet and gas mask before being sucked into the icy water. Dragged deep beneath the ship, he felt an intense pressure in his ears and realized he was going to die.

Unable to reach the surface and desperate to breathe, he gulped down mouthfuls of water. As he drowned, his panic subsided. A childlike, blissful security swept over him. Briggs pictured himself as a little boy, and thought of his mother tucking him into bed. But his state of peaceful resignation was interrupted. A great surge of water suddenly shot him to the surface.

Choking and spluttering, Briggs gasped down great lungfuls of air, and took in a scene of unimaginable horror. All around were blazing pools of oil. What remained of the *Hood* was 45m (150ft) away. Her bows were vertical in the sea, the guns in her forward turrets were disappearing fast into the water. Bizarrely, these guns had just fired a final salvo toward the *Bismarck*, perhaps triggered by an electric short-circuit, as the bow lurched wildly into the air.

As she sank, the *Hood* made a horrific hissing sound, as white-hot metal and bubbling, blistering paint and wood made contact with the icy water. The *Prince of Wales* sailed close by, nearly colliding with the wreckage. The bow of the *Hood* towered over her like a nightmarish spire.

Realizing he was close enough to be sucked down again by the whirlpool currents the huge sinking ship was making, Briggs swam away through the oily sea as hard as he could. All around were dozens of small wooden rafts which had floated away when the *Hood* capsized, and he hauled himself onto one.

Perched precariously on the raft, he turned to look at the *Hood*, but she had vanished. Now nothing remained except a small patch of blazing oil where the bow had been. Beneath the waters, the huge 42,672 tonne (42,000 ton) ship was beginning a last terrible journey to the ocean floor, 2,500m (8,000ft) below. Once the *Bismarck*'s guns had found their target, his ship had sunk in a mere three minutes.

❖

Briggs was still in terrible danger. Shells from *Bismarck* and *Prinz Eugen* were falling around the *Prince of Wales*, only yards away, and the oil that surrounded him could catch fire at any moment. As he paddled away from the oil, he looked for other survivors. Two were close by. All three paddled toward one another and held their rafts together by linking arms. On one raft was Midshipman Bill Dundas, who had been on the compass platform with Briggs. When the *Hood* capsized, he kicked his way out of a window and swam away from the ship.

The other man was Able Seaman Bob Tilburn, who had been manning a gun position at the side of the ship. His had been the luckiest escape. On deck, he had survived exploding ammunition lockers, and had been showered with falling debris and the bodies of men from the decks above. When the *Hood* capsized, he jumped into the water only to have the ship come down on top of him. Radio wiring had wrapped itself around his sea boots and he had cut himself free with a knife.

Alone in the ocean, the three men were now in danger of freezing to death. To stop them from falling asleep and dying of exposure, Dundas made them sing "Roll out the barrel" – a wartime pop song. Fortunately they did not have to wait too long for help to arrive. The British destroyer *Electra* had spotted the three men and was now heading toward them.

Ted Briggs was too cold to haul himself up to the ship and had to be lifted aboard. In *Electra*'s sick bay, frozen clothes were cut from his body and he was given rum to warm him up.

The *Electra* and three other ships had been sent to look for survivors. There was so little sign of life when they arrived at the scene of the sinking that they thought they must have gone off course.

Briggs, Dundas and Tilburn, and a few wooden rafts, were all that was left. The *Hood* had taken the rest of her 1,421 crew – from Vice-Admiral to engine room stoker – to the bottom of the North Atlantic.

After the ordeal

The destruction of the *Hood* stunned the British public. She was believed to be unsinkable, and many people in Britain remember the moment they heard the news as the single greatest shock of the war. Prime Minister Winston Churchill recalled: "*HMS Hood*. . . was one of our most cherished naval possessions. Her loss was a bitter grief."

A Royal Navy inquiry concluded the *Hood* had been sunk because her protective steel plating was too weak to defend her from plunging shells fired by the German battleships. Tragically, the *Hood* was due to have had all this strengthened in a major renovation, but this had been postponed when war broke out in 1939.

The *Bismarck* did not survive the exchange with *Hood* and *Prince of Wales* unscathed. Minor damage, including leaking fuel tanks, prompted her commander Admiral Lutjens to return to base, in the German-occupied French port of Brest. But on the journey back, *Bismarck* was attacked and crippled by British torpedo planes. Finally, on May 27, 1941, she was sunk by British battleships, a mere four days after her victory over the *Hood*.

Prinz Eugen survived the war, and was surrendered to the British in May 1945. She was handed over to the Americans, who used her for atomic bomb trials at Bikini Atoll in the Pacific. She eventually capsized and sank in December 1946.

The *Prince of Wales* was sunk in the Pacific Ocean by the Japanese Navy, later in 1941.

Following their rescue by the *Electra*, Ted Briggs and his crewmates were taken to Reykjavik, Iceland, and then flown back to England to be reunited with their families for one week's "survival leave". Briggs's mother received a telegram telling her he was safe, only an hour after radio reports announced that the *Hood* had sunk with little chance of survivors.

Briggs, Dundas and Tilburn all survived the war. Serving for 35 years in the British Royal Navy, Briggs rose to the rank of lieutenant. He now lives in Hampshire, and is a prominent member of the Hood Association – an organization set up to preserve the memory of his former ship. He still gives interviews to researchers and documentary producers, and in 2000 he appeared in a Discovery Channel documentary about the sinking of the *Hood*.

Also from Usborne True Stories

TRUE STORIES OF
ESCAPE

PAUL DOWSWELL

Finally, the night had come to take a
trip to the roof. Morris spent the day
beforehand trying to curb his restlessness.
What if the way up to the roof was
blocked? What if the ventilator motor
had been replaced after all? All their
painstaking work would be wasted. The
12 year sentence stretched out before
him. Then another awful thought
occurred. The holes in the wall would
be discovered eventually, and that would
mean even more years added on to
his sentence.

As well as locked doors, high walls and barbed
wire, many escaping prisoners also face savage dogs
and armed guards who shoot to kill. From Alcatraz
to Devil's Island, read the extraordinary tales of
people who risked their lives for their freedom.

Also from Usborne True Stories

TRUE STORIES OF
HEROES

PAUL DOWSWELL

His blood ran cold and Perevozchenko was seized by panic. He knew that his body was absorbing lethal doses of radiation, but instead of fleeing he stayed to search for his colleague. Peering into the dark through a broken window that overlooked the reactor hall, he could see only a mass of tangled wreckage.

By now he had absorbed so much radiation he felt as if his whole body was on fire. But then he remembered that there were several other men near to the explosion who might also be trapped . . .

From firefighters battling with a blazing nuclear reactor to a helicopter rescue team on board a fast-sinking ship, this is an amazingly vivid collection of stories about men and women whose extraordinary courage has captured the imagination of millions.